The Return Of The Santa Fe Super Chief

Douglas Folsom

A NOVEL

This book is a work of fiction. Names, characters, places, and incidents are the product of the author's imagination or are used fictitiously. Any resemblance to actual events, locales, or persons, living or dead, is coincidental.

ISBN: 148007473X
ISBN-13: 9781480074736
Library of Congress Control Number: 2012918999
CreateSpace Independent Publishing Platform
North Charleston, South Carolina

About the Author

Douglas Folsom is a filmmaker and ordained pastor who after spending years writing sermons, devoted the last few years to writing screenplays and novels. He grew up learning about railroads from his dad, the former general manager of transportation for Amtrak. Douglas presently lives with his wife and daughter in Lexington, Massachusetts.

Dedication

This book is dedicated to my dad, Deane R. Folsom, Sr.

The Super Chief Passing Rowe, New Mexico, 1965 by landscape and railroad artist Deane R. Folsom, Sr.

Table of Contents

Acknowledgements

I want to thank my dad for sharing his love of railroads with me when I was growing up and for giving our family the opportunity to experience a bit of the fading magic of long-distance train travel in the 1960s.

I'd like to thank three railroad consultants for their technical expertise, research, and editing: my dad, Deane R. Folsom Sr., former assistant general manager of the Boston and Maine Railroad and former general manager of transportation for Amtrak; Michael R. Weinman, managing director of PTSI Transportation and former official with Amtrak; and Bruce Heard, former vice president of Amtrak, West Coast.

A special thanks to the BNSF Railway for giving me permission to show all the Santa Fe Railway material in this book.

Thanks also to Avalon Rail Inc., and Lancaster and Chester Railway Company for help with research.

Thanks to Shun Lee Fong for his creative insights, editing, and encouragement.

Thanks to all those family and friends who read early drafts of the manuscript and screenplay: Cindy Folsom, Deane Folsom II, Cecilia Deane, Oris Folsom, Byron Bollas, James Burke, and James O'Keeffe. Thanks to David McFadzean for providing early coverage on the screenplay. Thanks to Steve Kennedy for his support and encouragement with this project. Thanks to Janet Batchler and her screenwriting class for helping me develop the original screenplay version of the story. Thanks to

Bianca Bezdek-Goodloe for her encouragement and legal help. Thanks to the CreateSpace creative team for their insights and support. And thanks to Steve Bock for our conversation many years ago over dinner at CPK.

And most of all, thanks to my wife, Renee Cutiongco Folsom, for her patience and loving support.

Photo Credits

Photos by Raymond H. Doss, courtesy Randy Doss: Front cover train, p. 24.

Photos reprinted with permission of BNSF Railway Company: pp. 16, 42, 70, 88, 104, 140, 162, 182.

Photos reprinted with permission of Xanterra Parks and Resorts, Inc.: pp. x, 80.

TURQUOISE
ROOM
Super Chief

Chapter One

THE VISITATION

Thanks for letting me take this seat; it's been an honor to hear your story. I must admit, if I may be so bold—and I say this with all compassion for your situation—before I came over here, I thought you had the look of someone who has struggled with forgiveness and was having a hard time moving forward with his life.

No, nothing in particular I saw—just my intuition. But then again, if we're honest with ourselves, who hasn't been hurt by others and struggled to forgive? The difference lies in how a person moves on.

Yes, I know what it's like to experience loss. I've had my fair share. In no way do I discount the loss and hardship you've been through. I've just found that, in order to move forward in life, we need to deal with our past—not dwell in it, just deal with it. From what you've told me, I'm not sure you have.

Hope? I think we all can use hope, and I'm sorry you don't have any.

The supernatural? Yes, I do believe there are forces at work in the world, beyond what we see. I think a bit of magic could break into your humdrum reality. I would encourage you there is more to the world than what you see with your eyes.

How do I know there is something beyond what we see? Hmm...I'm not sure if answering that directly will help. Are you one of those people who want answers without having to go through the journey? It's OK to admit it.

Yes. Yes, I thought so. Instead of answering that question for you, my friend, I want you to experience it for yourself and embrace the mystery. Let me tell you about a man named Roger Storm…No, I'm getting ahead of myself. Where to begin? Let's start at the railroad station…

It was a cold night by Los Angeles standards. The lit Art Deco front entrance of Union Station loomed large in the still night sky, its clock tower reading two thirty.

After the usual busy day of ushering about two hundred trains in and out of the City of Angels, the platform area and its twelve tracks showed no signs of activity. All was silent. Then, suddenly and mysteriously, *whoosh*—the final release of pressurized air from diesel locomotive brake cylinders and a fog of white steam enveloped the platform at track seven. This was odd because steam had not been used to heat and cool trains in many years. Where had it come from?

As the fog subsided, the form of a mysterious, elderly African American man emerged from the mist. Walking with a limp and carrying a cane, the mysterious man wore a Pullman Company train porter's outfit from the 1940s: starched white jacket, black tie, and visored pillbox cap. He smiled as he turned to survey the station—the smile of a man returning home. So many memories filled his mind.

Then he remembered something and looked down. He held a paper menu with a picture of a turquoise necklace on the front. It read, "Turquoise Room Menu, Santa Fe Super Chief."

He folded the menu into a paper airplane, raised it as high as his arm could reach, and, in a magical moment, he blew at the menu. It glided into the night sky, higher and higher until it disappeared out of sight. The man looked on, pleased.

* * *

The next morning in Malibu marked the start of a typical sunny California day—except for the magical floating menu still gliding in the sky. It finally began its descent, twirling down and then suddenly, smoothly gliding onto the porch of a quaint, two-story, Santa Fe adobe-style house. Modest by Malibu standards, the house stood nestled on a wooded hill with other small cottages nearby, a few hundred yards from the beach on a quarter-acre of ocean-view property.

The owner of the house, Roger Storm, jogged at nearby Point Dume Beach, a rather isolated area by Los Angeles standards. One-hundred-foot-high cliffs rose straight up from the shoreline with only a stairway providing entrance to the beach, restricting the access of the general public and would-be surfers. Roger liked living near one of the few places to get away from the Los Angeles crowds.

A fit-looking forty-five-year-old Caucasian man, Roger had the physique of a thirty-five-year-old. In fact, people occasionally mistook him for George Clooney. At first glance, one might believe he'd bought in wholeheartedly to the Los Angeles/Hollywood self-serving lifestyle, but it didn't suit him. He struggled with it and got frustrated when he or those close to him seemed to settle for superficiality. He would get bored, for instance, at the Hollywood parties his neighbors invited him to, like the one he'd attended the night before. So many people there seemed plastic and phony to him—concerned only about their appearances and careers. He could spot those types within a minute of conversation. Because Roger carried a confident demeanor, they would start asking him questions about what he did for a living, and when they found out that he wasn't involved in the entertainment industry and couldn't help them in their careers, they would move on to someone else. A film producer might carry the conversation a bit further to see if he was interested in investing in films, but would soon leave once Roger showed no interest. Or for those who needed an audience, they might stick around longer, but only to talk about themselves.

Sometimes the opposite type of encounter occurred where he was the person trying to escape. There might be a woman, usually an aspiring actress, who would make a pass at him. Even though he would mention he was in a committed relationship, she might become relentless, and he would have to find a creative way to escape the conversation. With such a population prevalent at the party the night before, Roger got bored and left early.

But now, jogging on the beach, he realized he couldn't judge those people at the party because he struggled with the same things himself. He seemed to always want the good things in life and enjoyed having a successful career and a beautiful woman at his side—like his thirty-five-year-old raven-haired fiancée, Brook Graham, jogging beside him. Still, he wondered if there should be something more. He thought maybe he should volunteer for a charity or at a church soup kitchen.

Roger also never felt Los Angeles was home. He could never get used to not having four seasons, like he'd experienced as a kid. No seasonal markers of fall foliage, winter snow, spring blooms, and summer warmth meant no sense of time passing. Los Angeles had two seasons: cool and cloudy with a mixture of smog, or hot and sunny with a mixture of smog. Everything in LA seemed in a time warp to him, years passing quickly with no signs of change. Once-famous actors appearing in the news with more wrinkles seemed the only indications of passing time. Where had his life gone?

So even though Roger lived the good life, if one looked closely, they might observe a hidden, almost imperceptible, lingering stress and unsettledness below the surface.

Brook, a confident career woman used to getting what she desired, wanted to use this time jogging to finalize her plan to have their wedding reception at the Beverly Hills Hotel. Because both her parents had died, Roger had offered to pay all the wedding expenses. That was something they had in common—both his parents had passed away also.

After she told him her ideas, Roger stopped in his tracks and blurted out, "The Beverly Hills Hotel?"

"It's always been my dream to have my wedding there," she said, turning. "There's not a problem, is there?"

Roger had compassion for her because he knew she'd grown up poor, and he wanted to make her wedding day nice, but this seemed unnecessarily extravagant.

"Nothing, except…it's very expensive."

Brook suddenly looked up ahead, narrowed her eyes, and said, "Loser to the porch has to make breakfast."

"OK, babe."

Brook broke out ahead as she went into a full sprint. Roger shook his head and smirked. He liked her spunk. It was what first attracted him to her when they first met at the tennis club. He invited her to play a game, and she said she would only play with him if he were prepared to lose. She never let him forget that she won that first match. He had to keep gently reminding her, however, that she hadn't won since, which only served to spark her competitive spirit more.

With all this in mind, he confidently paced himself behind her. She reached the metal stairway first, and he followed her up to the top of the sea cliff. After jogging on a trail through the state park and up a side road, they approached Roger's house, where the menu had landed. As they got nearer, she looked back at him and again broke into a full sprint, but he passed her and climbed the porch steps first. Their faces expressed both playful and competitive grins as they paced to catch their breath.

Just as Roger stuck his key in the front door, he saw something vaguely familiar lying near the doormat: the Turquoise Room menu. He paused and picked it up, looked at it, and stiffened. The Turquoise symbol and the words were from a part of his life he wanted to forget.

Brook wasn't watching him. She was focused on her thighs, still wondering whether she should go ahead with the liposuction surgery. Roger had told her a number of times she looked great and not to do it, but she felt insecure. On top of that, some of her girlfriends at the tennis club were encouraging her to do it.

"That's bizarre," he said.

"What?" She looked up.

"Nothing. Just some old train menu."

Roger crumpled the menu and opened the door. Once inside, he threw the menu into a wastebasket. Seeing the crushed menu land in the trash, Brook bent down and could just read the words "Serving Famous Super Chief French Toast."

As they sat on a bench in the foyer and began removing their running shoes, Roger picked up their wedding conversation. "I was just thinking of something more simple for the reception."

"'Simple?'" Brook gasped. "I told you…"

"I know," Roger interjected. "Nothing but the best for you."

She thrust her dirty socks into her running shoes and slapped them onto the floor tile. "Exactly. And a woman is particular about her wedding."

Roger couldn't resist giving her a hard time. "You're particular about everything!"

She playfully poked him in the stomach.

Roger got up and led her toward the living room. She picked up a soft pillow from the bench behind him and tossed it after him. It missed Roger and hit a silver plaque on a wall, knocking it uneven. It read, "Roger Storm, Allied Sky Airways Marketing Executive of the Year, 2010."

"Sorry." She giggled as she placed her hand over her mouth to stifle a laugh.

Roger shook his head and grinned while he leveled the plaque back in place.

Mission-style furniture and accents of Southwestern warmth—Navajo and Hopi paintings and rugs—filled the wood-floored interior. Models of commercial passenger jets lay scattered on the side tables, and between two Navajo paintings, a framed contemporary poster read, "Allied Sky Airways—the only way to travel!"

As he finished adjusting the plaque, Brook snuggled up behind him, wrapping her arms around him.

He turned around in her embrace. "What am I getting myself into?" he asked. As they swayed in each other's arms, they nudged the side table behind them, bumping a plastic model plane off the edge onto the rug.

"The ride of your life!" Brook said seductively.

"Oh, yeah?"

They kissed passionately. The plane rested, unnoticed, upside down on the rug.

* * *

Dressed in his business attire, Roger cleaned the dishes after breakfast. Brook, also in business attire, put the finishing touches on her makeup.

Roger yawned as he washed the dishes but quickly became attentive as he noticed a strange plate designed with a Mimbreno Indian pattern. He looked at it curiously. It looked strangely familiar, but it wasn't his.

He showed it to Brook. "Is this your plate?" he asked.

"No. It was out on your deck table," she said.

Roger looked confused but put the plate into the dishwasher. At the kitchen table, Brook stuffed her used towel into her gym bag, and then placed the bag's shoulder harness over her, getting ready to leave. Then she reached for some brochures on the tabletop that read, "Beverly Hills Hotel."

The doorbell rang, and Roger looked at the kitchen clock. "A few minutes early; that's a first," Roger said. "I'll go out with you."

As Brook exited the kitchen, Roger downed his coffee and then followed her into the living room. When they reached the front door, Roger picked up his black suitcase and yawned again.

"You have your sleeping pills?" Brook asked.

Roger nodded.

She handed him the hotel brochures. "Just wait till you see the pictures of the honeymoon suite!"

"I'll look at it on the plane." He shoved the brochures into his suitcase, grabbed his laptop, and followed her to the door.

Outside, Brook waved and sped away in her BMW as Roger stood in the driveway, waving back.

Roger approached the waiting limousine, which had its trunk lid raised. He rounded the rear of the limo, and came with surprise upon the mysterious man from the train station in his porter's outfit, holding his cane. Roger looked quizzically at him.

"Eddie's off today," the mysterious man assured him.

Roger thought a moment and nodded.

Cane still in hand, the mysterious man took Roger's bag with his other hand and set it in the trunk. Roger kept his laptop with him as he got in the car.

A few minutes later, the mysterious man was driving the limousine while Roger dozed in the backseat. A tinted window separated them.

Roger's cell phone rang, waking him. He looked at its screen: "Airport Limo Service."

"Yes?" he answered.

"Mr. Storm," the limo service operator said, "our driver has been waiting in front of your house."

"He already picked me up," Roger said.

"No sir. I have Eddie on the other line. He's still waiting."

"That's impossible," Roger said. "I'm..." His voice trailed off as he looked out the window. The passing view was not what he'd been expecting. Instead of being near LAX, the limo was heading on Alameda Street in downtown Los Angeles.

Roger lowered the phone and called out to the driver, "Hey, where are we? This isn't near the airport."

The driver was silent.

"Stop the car now!" Roger yelled.

With Union Station looming above it, the limousine came to an abrupt stop, right by a sign that read, "No Stopping." Rush-hour cars and pedestrians filled the surrounding street and sidewalks.

Inside the limousine, the mysterious driver locked onto Roger's eyes in the rearview mirror. "Do you want to start an adventure today?"

"What?" Roger asked.

"I've brought you here for a reason, Roger."

"Who are you?" Roger asked with a mixture of fear and anger. He tried to get out of the car, but the doors were locked.

"You can call me Mr. Chapman," the mysterious man said.

"Look, Mr. Chapman, you're freaking me out. You better let me out of here, now!"

Mr. Chapman shook his head. "I want you to bring back the Super Chief, Roger."

"The Super Chief? Oh, so you're the one who put the menu by the door."

"And the Mimbreno plate," Mr. Chapman said, chuckling. "Just some added personal touches."

Roger tried to control his anger using the technique he'd recently learned in his anger management class, by taking deep breaths and breathing slowly. "If you know what's good for you," Roger said slowly and coolly, "you'll open these doors now, and I won't press any charges."

Outside the limousine, a cop knocked on the trunk to hurry it along. He couldn't see through the tinted windows. "Yo! Move the car!" he yelled.

But Mr. Chapman and Roger continued their stare-off in the rearview mirror.

"I was hoping you would be more open," Mr. Chapman finally said.

"Let me out!"

After a long period of continued staring, Mr. Chapman saw that Roger wasn't close to budging. *Click!* The doors unlocked.

Mr. Chapman got out and limped to the back of the car. Roger cautiously opened his door, got out, and joined him there.

"The old station still looks pretty good, don't you think?" Mr. Chapman asked.

"Just give me my suitcase."

Mr. Chapman tried to hand Roger a train ticket. "I got you a train ticket to San Francisco to get to your meeting."

Roger looked down, saw what it was, and scoffed. He wouldn't take it. *Who is this guy?* Roger thought. *The audacity.*

"Why would a VP of marketing for an airline…travel by train?" Roger chided him.

"You know, Roger: to get back to your roots," Mr. Chapman said with a penetrating stare.

Roger ignored him and motioned with his hand for Mr. Chapman to open the trunk. Using a remote key, Chapman popped it open. Roger reached in and grabbed his suitcase.

"If I wasn't in such a hurry, I'd have you arrested," Roger said. He briskly strode away to the nearby taxi stand and hailed a cab. "I need to get to LAX A-SAP!" Roger said.

The cabdriver nodded. Roger hopped in the back, and the cab started moving. Roger, still freaked out, glared out the window as the cab passed Mr. Chapman, who gave Roger a knowing look. The cab merged into traffic.

Mr. Chapman looked heavenward, nodded, then said, "I know: Plan B."

Roger tried to collect himself in the cab and then placed a call on his cell phone. Roger's assistant, twenty-eight year old Dena Walker, answered in her office at Allied Sky Airways. A very pretty Native American woman, Dena was conscientious and very loyal to Roger.

"Hi, Roger."

"Dena, I missed the flight."

"Oh…everything OK?"

"Yeah. Tell them we'll have to push back the meeting an hour."

"Sure thing. Anything else?"

"Can you text me a margarita?" Roger tried to joke.

Dena laughed.

Roger hung up, looked out the window, and tried to calm down. The whole episode with the limo driver felt like something out of a bad dream. It was so surreal, nobody would ever believe it. He kept thinking, *Who was that guy?*

The cab pulled up to the LAX terminal, and Roger quickly paid the driver and bolted out, worried he wouldn't even make the next flight.

After going through an unusually light security line, Roger ran down the Allied Sky Airways concourse past several gates, lugging his carry-on. He thought how typical it seemed that whenever he was in a hurry, his plane was assigned to the last gate. Finally he reached his gate and ran onto the passenger ramp. He panted as he just made it onto the plane in time and the flight attendant closed the door behind him. He put his bags in the overhead bin and sat down in seat 2B, a first-class aisle seat.

A passenger in window seat 2A next to Roger sat turned away from him, facing the window sleeping, a blanket up to his shoulders and a Brooklyn Dodgers baseball hat pulled low over his face. Roger sighed with relief, but he was still reeling from his crazy morning. He thought maybe the sleeping pills had something to do with it and wondered if he had been hallucinating. Until this last year, he hadn't been used to taking any sort of medication. In fact, he felt ashamed about it. But the sleeplessness, anger, and depression had taken a toll on him. Now, he kept wondering what Mr. Chapman had meant about getting back to his roots.

A few minutes after takeoff, Roger began to relax. A TV newscast played on the small TV screen in front of him. Roger watched it with airline earphones on and began nodding off. He turned down the sound and closed his eyes.

Suddenly a train horn blared in his earphones, startling him awake.

On the TV screen, a 1950s-style commercial for The Santa Fe Railway Super Chief appeared. Roger looked at nearby TV monitors, but they were all playing other programs. He pushed the channel-control buttons on his seat, but his channel wouldn't change.

The film narrator on the earphones said, "Just how comfortable can train travel be? Well, here's the one and only answer to that question: The new Super Chief, flagship of Santa Fe's great fleet of streamliners. All-private-room train, grand hotel on rails, in daily service between Chicago and Los Angeles…"

Wide eyed, Roger ripped off his earphones. *Am I going crazy?* he wondered.

The Flight Attendant came with his lunch. "Would you care for a meal, Mr. Storm?"

Roger wavered, then amenably put down his tray table. The attendant served a plain-looking lasagna and tiny salad in white plastic dishes on a paper mat and plastic tray. Roger looked less than enthusiastic about his lunch.

The passenger seated next to him chuckled and said, "They call this first-class?"

That voice sounded familiar, and Roger did a double take when he saw the passenger seated beside him. *Mr. Chapman!*

Mr. Chapman continued in a casual manner. "Nothing like the old days on the Super Chief, where they made the food fresh on board and served it on china, with real silverware, linen tablecloths, and fresh-cut flowers."

Roger collected himself, turned to Mr. Chapman, and said pointedly, "Are you going to make a living of following me around?"

"You remember the French toast, Roger?" Mr. Chapman asked, ignoring the question.

"So what if I do?" Roger said impatiently.

"Ahh, whatever happened to the slower pace of life—where we used to enjoy the journey?" Mr. Chapman ruminated.

Roger looked the other way, shaking his head. "I'm not getting away from you, am I?"

"Not until you hear me out."

Roger again tried to practice the relaxation breathing exercise from his anger management class. After a moment, he asked, "What do you want?"

"I told you." Mr. Chapman perked up. "Bring back the Super Chief, for one trip from Chicago to Los Angeles."

"Why me?"

"Who's the one person who would be most honored by this trip?"

"Are you talking about my dad?"

Mr. Chapman nodded and winked.

"Why would I want to do that? No way."

"It's not just that. It will help others also."

"I'm not into trains. Go find some wealthy rail fan." Roger took a bite of the lasagna. Unimpressed, he set his fork down.

"It has to be you," Mr. Chapman continued. "And you need to restore the original, consist of nine cars and two diesel engines in warbonnet colors, to their original gleaming condition. And by the way, don't forget the Pleasure Dome car. That's my favorite. You know, the one with the Turquoise Room in it."

Looking incredulous, Roger asked, "Anything else?"

"You need to have five-star Fred Harvey-quality food on board. And hire some of the original staff. I have a list here. They need to be honored during the trip."

Mr. Chapman handed Roger a list, handwritten on a piece of Santa Fe Chief stationery.

"And there's a few other people you need to get on board," Mr. Chapman added. "They're also on the list. Don't tell them about me. That would just confuse things."

Roger looked at the list. It read, "Wixie Wilson, Curtis Gibson, Henry Wellington, Chicago, IL; Chester Young, Greensboro, VT; Violet Briggs, Beaufort, SC; Dena Walker, LA, CA; Janet Thompson, LA, CA."

"My assistant, Dena, is on here? The rest live all over the country."

"You'll figure it out," Mr. Chapman encouraged him. "And you need to hurry, because you have to arrange things so it arrives in Los Angeles on May 2 of next year."

Roger, wanting to challenge this perceived bluff, took a moment and said, "Hmm. And what if I don't?"

"If you don't," Mr. Chapman replied, "you will continue to live in misery."

"But I'm not miserable," Roger insisted. He tried to hand back the list, but Mr. Chapman wouldn't take it. Roger became emphatic. "I am not doing this."

Mr. Chapman ignored his remarks again and said, "Something else, Roger: don't go raising the money elsewhere. The investment needs to come from you, from your own heart."

The flight attendant approached Roger, concerned. "Is, uh…something wrong, Mr. Storm?"

A little annoyed by the question, Roger turned toward her. "No. We're just having a conversation."

The flight attendant, speechless, looked at the empty window seat. Roger turned toward the window and was dumbfounded. *Where did he go? She must think I'm crazy*, he thought.

310

Chapter Two

GENERATIONAL INFLUENCES

I hope I've gotten your attention.

Yes, the flight attendant did wonder about Roger. Wouldn't you?

How did Mr. Chapman get on and off the plane? Or was he a figment of Roger's imagination? Hmm... there you go, wanting to jump ahead without enjoying the journey. Before I answer that, let me first share a bit about how Brook reacted to Roger's new "friend" and give a little more background about Roger and his family...

Roger and Brook biked along the cement pathway near the pier on Santa Monica Beach as a few other bicyclists and joggers passed by. Roger kept thinking about Mr. Chapman. *Should I tell her?* he wondered. *If I can't talk to her about this, then why are we engaged?* He finally decided to take the plunge. After sharing what had happened, he waited for her response.

"Voices? You heard voices?"

He started to feel he'd made a mistake. Her tone was not very understanding. "I didn't say I heard voices. It was a guy with a voice."

"And what did he look like?"

"Nelson Mandela."

Brook seemed only half-interested in Roger's story. "And he told you to bring back a train?"

"The Santa Fe Super Chief. They used to call it 'The Train of the Stars' because all the Hollywood stars would take it."

"This is about your dad, isn't it?" Brook countered.

Roger was taken aback by her response, lost control of his bike, and went into the sand, falling off. Brook stopped her bike. Amid the silent tension, he got up and brushed the sand off himself, embarrassed and angry.

"Guess I shouldn't have brought up your dad," Brook said.

"Guess not," Roger agreed. Noticing sand had gotten inside his helmet and into his hair, he took his helmet off, shook it, and brushed the sand out of his hair.

He started to go again but saw Brook's demeanor change as she looked toward the beach restroom building, not moving. He drew his bike up close to her, and they stood side by side, straddling their bikes.

"What?" Roger asked.

She still didn't move. He leaned nearer to her, and she turned toward him, hesitated, and then said, "When Mom and I lived out of the car, we'd wash here."

Roger, taken aback, tried to comfort her. "I'm sorry. I should have suggested somewhere else." He put his arm around her.

She wiped a tear from her face and collected herself. "It's OK." She changed the topic back to their previous conversation. "So what are you going to do?"

"About what?" he asked.

"The train."

"Nothing," Roger said. "Besides, I need to focus on the wedding."

Brook caressed his arm and looked alluringly into his eyes. "Speaking of which," she said, "the guest list is pushing four hundred."

Roger was determined to stand his ground on this issue. They had discussed it many times. "Honey, we agreed to keep it at three hundred."

"No. You suggested it, but I didn't necessarily agree to it."

"That's not true. You said—"

"Well, I changed my mind."

"Look," Roger began but stopped, so he would not escalate the argument. They stared each other down for a few moments in silence.

Brook pouted and abruptly started ahead on her bike without him. Roger shook his head and started to catch up. He wondered why so many of their conversations felt like emotional roller coasters, taking dramatic turns on a dime.

* * *

Later that evening, Roger sat alone in the glow of a living room lamp in his boxers, hair disheveled, holding a beer. He felt relieved to have some time to himself after getting more of the silent treatment from Brook earlier in the day. He'd become accustomed to her mood swings when she didn't get what she wanted. He was used to women with mood swings. His mother had always been unpredictable. Maybe the drama of their erratic behavior made him feel alive—at least it felt familiar—but he knew deep down that he desired peace and calm. The drama and high maintenance had taken an emotional toll on him. He wondered, though, what he would do with a woman who was peaceful and consistently loving. Could he handle it, or would he get bored?

He looked at the wall clock. What am I doing up at three o'clock in the morning? he thought. He rose to get another beer. As he walked along the edge of the Navajo rug in front of the couch, he accidently kicked the upside-down plastic model plane that had fallen off the side table only a few days before. He picked up the plane and set it back on the coffee table next to an old photo of a handsome man and a black-haired woman—his stepfather, Ken, and his mother, Marlene.

Roger sat back down on the couch and gazed at the photo as he sipped what was left of his stale beer. He focused on his mother's picture.

It brought him back to the memory of the day she took him from his father and their quaint Southwestern style house in Glorieta, New Mexico, outside Santa Fe. It was 1969, and when he was seven years old. His mother made sure he was dressed in a suit and tie for their trip. Before they left, young Roger looked at a photo, placed on the mantel of the adobe-style fireplace, of his mother in happier days with his dad, George Wickersham. He lifted it off the mantel and held it.

Roger remembered his mother rush in to get him. At thirty-five, she was dressed in a sultry outfit designed to attract a man's attention. In fact, aside from the 1960s clothing and hairdo, she looked similar to Roger's fiancée, Brook.

* * *

Marlene was an enigma. She was very guarded about her past, even with Roger after he grew up. Roger never knew what really went on between his parents. She only made reference that she was from Brazil, but she said she had no family. How she ended up in Santa Fe, no one knew. Some things she would never reveal, but she seemed to be running from something.

She met her husband George seven years earlier when she worked as a waitress at a local diner George frequented in Santa Fe. It was unclear why such an exotic, complicated woman would work in a diner, much less pursue George except that he appeared safe and had a steady job as a locomotive engineer. Perhaps he was just a ticket out of the restaurant life for her.

Marlene observed George from a distance when his group would be served in a different section of the diner. He initially appeared awkward to her, but in an endearing way. When he came into the diner, he often wore his standard engineer's coveralls, a pinstriped BK75 hat, black-framed glasses, and a classic red bandana around his neck, which engineers hadn't worn since the 1930s, when they ran steam locomotives and had to protect themselves from hot cinders getting under their collars. Other engineers would often tease George about wearing the bandana, but he wanted to look like the engineers he'd admired as a little kid. He was a bit of a big kid, hoping to find a simple, loving woman like his mother was. An only child, he had kind parents who brought him up in New Hampshire, where his dad was a pastor. His parents introduced him to trains by frequently taking short trips into Boston via the Boston & Maine Railroad. One day they passed a travel agency on Newbury Street that had a full window display enticing people to travel out West on the Santa Fe Super Chief. Young George petitioned his dad to pick up some brochures for him, and he became enamored with the Southwest and the Santa Fe Railway ever since.

Ever since George was a little kid, he dreamed of one day being an engineer on the Santa Fe, so when he graduated from the University of Maine, off he went. His parents initially were concerned for him because he had never had a girlfriend and he tended to stay to himself and was socially awkward. But after a few months, some of their fears were relieved when they heard that their son made friends on the railway. Still, their prayers for their son to meet a woman went unmet.

George was heartbroken when his parents died in a car crash a few years later. Even though he loved working for the railway, he seemed a bit lost in his life. That's when he met Marlene.

Even though George had a lot of boyish qualities, he had a strong side also. He had noticed the pretty new waitress at the diner a couple of times, but she hadn't served his table. He was hoping that would change the next time he came to the restaurant. His chance came on his next visit in a way he would not have imagined. Before he entered the restaurant, he observed her in the parking lot, dressed in her uniform, being harassed by a muscular biker trying to grab her. She screamed for the man to let go, but he wouldn't release his hold on her arm.

George came over. "Let the lady go!"

"Over your dead body. Mind your own business."

"I said to let her go." George grabbed the guy and threw him to the ground. When the biker tried to charge him, George punched him several times and knocked him out. He returned to Marlene, who was shaken.

"Are you OK?"

She nodded and leaned into his chest. "Thank you so much."

George was flustered to have such a beautiful woman in his arms. The scent of her perfume and the touch of her soft hands on his arms made him want to hold her for a long time. On her part, she felt safe in his strong embrace.

She made sure that George sat in her section thereafter. She gave him plenty of hints that she would like to go out with him, and within a couple of weeks they began dating.

George never outgrew his childlike enthusiasm for trains. Before he met Marlene, he had built three model-railroad sets on plywood tables in his home—O, HO, and N scale—that took up two bedrooms and the garage.

His Santa Fe–style adobe house sat on a high desert hill sprinkled with pinyon trees and few houses nearby. When Marlene visited his house for the first time, she was struck how remote it was compared to her small apartment near downtown Santa Fe. George prepared her beforehand about the train sets. He brought her in through the side kitchen door and guided her down a short hallway.

"Why do you have all these different sets?" she asked, trying not to appear too negative.

He led her into the first bedroom. "One for each scale."

"What does 'scale' mean?"

"The different sizes. The scale refers to the proportions of the model train compared to the real train. So in here are the larger O scale trains that are 1 to 48 in proportion." He noticed her blank expression. "The real train is 48 times bigger than this size."

She moved her head in feigned agreement, trying to show interest. Inwardly, however, she wondered what she was getting herself into—especially if she decided to date him seriously. Still, she did find his enthusiasm charming, and she liked the way his short-sleeved shirt highlighted his prominent muscles. "That's the size train I see when people put a track on the floor around a Christmas tree."

"That's right. Since O scale is larger, small kids have an easier time using them. The challenge is that you need more space to have a nice set."

Marlene nodded as she followed a narrow portion of the table that ran through the bedroom doorway and spilled out onto a larger table in the living room. "So you can't even close the bedroom door?"

"Don't really have a need to."

Marlene nodded in disbelief but continued to try to look interested. She thought it a bit peculiar that a double bed, bureau, and couch occupied the other half of the living room.

"Why is there a bed in the living room?"

"Oh, that's where I sleep. I like to be near the fireplace."

"But why not sleep in a bedroom?"

"I put the other set in there."

She observed another set through an open door leading to the other bedroom. "And what's the scale in that room?"

"Oh, that's N scale—the smallest. It has a proportion of 1 to 160. They've recently started making more of these. It's great because you can make a huge set, but the rolling stock is a little too small and delicate for small kids and elderly folks to handle. Let me show you my HO scale set in the garage." He led her through the kitchen again to another door that led to the garage.

"Why not a set in the kitchen?" she asked lightheartedly.

"Have to eat." He gave her a wink.

In the garage, she found the HO scale set that was the middle size of the three scales with proportions of 1 to 87. This set included life-like mountains, tunnels, and a town.

"This scale makes a nice size because it's big enough for kids to play with, and it doesn't use up as much room as the O scale. Let me show you what I love to do." He plugged in the set, which produced lights in the buildings. He turned off the room lights, so the miniature town glowed in the darkness. George turned the knob on the transformer and a lit passenger train circled around the model village. For George, the train set gave him comfort from the real world—a world he found unpredictable and not always easy to manage.

As Marlene watched the model train glide through the dark and observed George's excitement, she thought about all the different interests men had and how women often needed to adapt to those interests to make a relationship work. Part of her resented that dynamic in romantic relationships, but she figured she could find a way to put up with model railroading.

She did determine though, that if she was going to go forward with the relationship, something had to be done to limit this hobby. She would later demand, as a stipulation before getting married, that he only have one set in the garage. He settled on the HO scale.

This was a bit of the relational background of Roger's parents, Marlene and George.

* * *

Roger continued gazing at the picture of his mother and stepfather, Ken, late that night in his house in Malibu. He reached over for the plastic model plane on the coffee table. As he held it, he kept thinking about that fateful day as a child in 1969 when he stood in front of the fireplace at his home in Glorieta, New Mexico—holding the picture of his dad, George, and his mother, Marlene. He remembered how the suit his mother made him wear felt uncomfortable—he particularly didn't like the tight collar and tie around his neck.

After Marlene rushed in, she snatched the picture out of her son's hand and tossed it back on the mantel. She led young Roger to the door and said, "I told you, honey, we have to go now, while Daddy's away."

They waited outside the small, simple, Santa Fe-style adobe house with three large suitcases. Marlene knelt, tucked in Roger's shirt, and straightened his tie. As she did so, the boy noticed a black-and-blue mark on the inside part of her upper arm. A train horn blew in the distance.

"Nice Mr. Storm works for the airlines," Marlene said, "and he's going to take us to Los Angeles on the plane—first class! Isn't that exciting?" She took out her compact mirror and checked her makeup.

"Nothing but the best," Marlene said to herself.

"Is Daddy going to come?" young Roger asked.

"No. I told you, honey: you need to trust your Mommy."

"But why isn't Daddy going to say good-bye to me?"

"He thought this was the best way for us to leave."

An expensive car pulled up, and out came Ken Storm, a handsome, blond thirty-five-year-old in a sharp business suit. He held the same plastic model plane Roger still had all those years later, and he handed it to young Roger.

"Hey, buddy," Ken said. "I thought you might like this."

Young Roger took it, disinterested.

"What do you say, honey?" Marlene reminded her son.

"Thank you," young Roger stammered.

"You're welcome!" Ken said. He flashed a dashing smile and tousled young Roger's hair. Then he picked up the suitcases and put them in the car. Young Roger climbed into the backseat, and Ken closed the door behind him. Marlene stood outside the car, waiting for Ken to open her door. Before opening it, Ken looked at Marlene, and she winked at him.

Young Roger watched this exchange and then looked sullenly down at the plastic model plane. Suddenly, the boy bolted out the car door and started running down the dirt road. Ken turned the car around and followed.

About one hundred yards up the road, young Roger turned down a desert path, which led out to a plateau scattered with small pinyon trees overlooking the railroad tracks in the distance. When Ken stopped the car where the boy entered the path, Marlene took off her high heels and chased after him.

Young Roger tripped along the path and dusty red soil covered his suit. Undeterred, he sprang back up and his destination came into focus: a rustic homemade bench made out of pinyon wood at the end of the path, fifty yards away. Somehow the boy thought that things would be all right if he could get there.

"Roger! Come here, Honey. Don't go there!" Her soft hand snatched his arm to stop him. She tried to keep her cool and stay calm as she glanced back at Ken, who was now standing beside the car in the distance. She noticed her son's dusty suit and started to brush him off. "Look what you've done."

"I don't want to go, Mommy! Where's Daddy?" Another train whistle blew in the distance.

She almost lost her temper. "I told you. We have to go!"

Young Roger noticed the shoulder strap to his mother's dress fell, revealing more of the deep bruise on her arm.

"What happened to your arm, Mommy?"

She quickly pulled up her strap as she continued to clean him up. She straightened his tie and removed more dust from his white shirt. She hesitated, deep in thought. She looked back at Ken, who was now starting to walk toward them.

Marlene straightened her son in front of her, holding onto his shoulders. "Your Daddy did it."

"Why would Daddy hit you?"

"Never mind—that's why we have to go. You need to trust me." She heard Ken's steps coming closer and nervously primped her hair before turning to him.

"What seems to be the problem?" Ken said with a slight smile.

"Oh, he just got excited and confused. He'll be all right." She put her arm around the boy. "Won't you, honey?" Young

Roger nodded shyly, but turned away momentarily when he heard the train horn again in the distance.

Ken bent down in front of Roger. “Well, that’s good because if we don’t go now, we won’t have time to stop for ice cream before the trip. What do you say, buddy…Time to go?”

The boy nodded and leaned in closer to his mother. She smiled at Ken and they walked back to the car. Young Roger returned to the back seat. He picked up the model airplane and rested it on his lap.

Roger came back to the present day as he held the plastic model plane in his hands. He looked at it a second, yawned, and then set it back on the table. He lay down to sleep on the couch. *No more beer*, he thought. *What did Chapman mean when he said I would continue to live in misery? What does he know?* Mr. Chapman was surely getting under Roger’s skin.

Chapter Three

DECISIONS

Well, Marlene might have had a good reason to leave George Wickersham like that. As you say, she had a bruise on her arm...but I'll get to more about that later. I want to move on for now.

Roger had a lot of life-changing decisions facing him. I'm sure you can relate to that. What would you have done in his position?

Go to a psychiatrist! That's one answer. Like you, Roger had a lot of potential change facing him. He didn't like it either—most people don't. Maybe you can relate to how reluctant Roger was to make decisions.

The next morning Roger sat in his office opening his mail at Allied Sky Airways Corporate Headquarters in Santa Monica. Interior glass walls surrounded his office, allowing him to observe activity outside his walls. On slow days like this, he would occasionally glance up from his work and watch people pass by. He wondered how many of the employees were trying to look busy but were not really interested in their work. He thought maybe they felt like him—just going through the motions. He turned and looked out the window at the beautiful view of the Santa Monica skyline with the ocean beyond. He noticed the fog, or the "marine layer," as the Angelinos liked to call it, starting to blow in toward shore.

Roger turned his attention once again to the mail. He opened a card and shook his head. The invitation read, "You're Invited! Allied Sky Airways Christmas Party, Friday, December 7, 7 p.m. At Union Station, The Fred Harvey Dining Room." Roger looked up and kept holding the invitation, flipping it in his hand. Dena came in and set a folder on his desk.

"Do you know anything about the Santa Fe Super Chief?" Roger asked.

She looked briefly startled, composed herself, and shook her head. "No."

Roger continued his investigation. "Aren't you on the planning team for the Christmas party?"

"Yes."

"Since when was the venue changed to Union Station?"

"I suggested it would be a good change. Plenty of space, nice surroundings, and catering is a breeze! Is there a problem?" she asked.

"No. It's no big deal," Roger said. Then another thought came to his mind. "Hey, you haven't noticed a guy who looks like Nelson Mandela hanging around, have you?"

"No. Why?" Dena asked, looking perplexed.

"Oh, nothing."

Dena slowly left his office, still looking confused.

Roger opened a package and pulled out two books, and inspected the box. It had no return address. He looked again at the covers of the books: *The Super Chief: The Train of the Stars* and *Santa Fe: The Chief Way*. He opened the first book to a photo of a man relaxing on a sleeping-car sofa. The caption beneath the photo read, "Dream in the Pleasure Dome, Relax in Luxurious Lounges, Dine in the Exquisite Turquoise Room." In spite of himself, Roger was curious and kept reading.

A loud voice interrupted his trance. "What's this? Missing our meeting to look at train pictures?"

Roger looked up to see his boss, Jack King, the president and chief operating officer of Allied Sky Airways, hovering over his shoulder. An A-type, workaholic micromanager, King felt insecure and threatened by Roger's abilities. It didn't take a detective to see from the blood vessels in King's nose that he enjoyed the bottle more than a bit too much.

Roger put the book aside. "Ahh, the meeting. I forgot. Sorry."

King ignored the apology; he was excited to get Roger's approval on what he thought was a brilliant idea. "Further thoughts on my idea?"

"With all due respect..." Roger hesitated, choosing his words carefully, "I don't think it works. It's hard enough to come up with an ad campaign on how we're a budget-friendly airline when we're charging extra for baggage and food already."

King's face turned flush. "So you're not on board?"

"No, sir," Roger said.

"And your alternative?"

"I think we should find a way to promote 'enjoying the journey.'"

King crossed over to close the door. "People don't care about comfort," he said in a patronizing tone. "They just want speed, and we have to make them think it's cheap. How else do you explain why we can keep nibbling our seat pitch, and the customers keep putting up with it?"

King looked at another of Roger's marketing awards on the wall, secretly envying his talents. "Y'know, Roger, marketing awards are like yesterday's newspaper. I need people with fresh ideas. Think on that. And you better get to that media luncheon in Monrovia."

Roger nodded, and King left. Roger put his hands in his pockets, looking for his keys. Dena observed his agitation and entered the office.

"Dena, have you seen…"

Dena walked over to the corner of his desk, picked up his keys, and jingled them at him. "What would you do without me?" she asked with a flirtatious look.

Roger shook his head, smiled, took the keys from her, and rushed out.

* * *

On his way to Monrovia, Roger reminded himself not to lose his cool while driving. Tailgaters frequently upset him, along with drivers who sped and cut him off. *Sure,* he'd tried to convince himself in the past, *everyone gets upset with reckless drivers.* But after he almost got into an accident because of his own road rage a few months back, he started going to the anger management class. He wondered why his fuse could be so short at times.

Roger drove his light blue BMW 6 Series convertible from the 10 Freeway to the 110 with no incidents during that warm afternoon drive. When he got to Pasadena, he decided to go east on Colorado Boulevard to Monrovia instead of getting on the 210 Freeway. He slowed to a stop and revved his engine as he waited behind a line of cars for a red light up ahead at the intersection of Colorado Boulevard and Altadena Drive.

A store to the right caught his attention: Original Whistle Stop Trains. The light turned green, and he turned in and parked his BMW in front of the store. He sat there, transfixed. Then he exited his car and went inside.

Upon entering he found himself standing in front of an elaborate train set. He smiled as he saw two model, HO scale, Santa Fe Super Chief F-7 engines running along the track.

He flashed back to 1971, when, at nine years old, he rode inside the real Super Chief engine cab with his dad, George Wickersham, forty-five at the time. George wore his standard engineer's coveralls, Kromer pinstriped cap, and his favorite red bandana. His black-framed glasses had fogged up, so he had to clean them off.

It had been two years since Marlene took young Roger away. He and his mother lived in Los Angeles with Ken. Marlene only let young Roger be with his dad because she and Ken were on their honeymoon. Young Roger and George had just spent two weeks together in Glorieta, New Mexico, and were on the return trip to Los Angeles. They had just a few more hours to be with each other before Marlene would meet them at Union Station, Los Angeles.

Young Roger was excited—as just about as any kid would be—to ride in a real engine cab. The only other time he had been this up-close to an engine was when his dad took him on a tour of a parked train in a rail yard when he was five-years old. Young Roger especially remembered that day because he still had the two pictures his dad took of him: one with him standing in front of the engine and the other one with him sitting in the front seat of the cab.

George had not gotten clearance for his son to ride in the cab with him on this trip. He reasoned it was better to ask for forgiveness if caught, rather than to ask for permission beforehand and possibly be turned down. George worked out of Albuquerque, either east to La Junta, Colorado, or west to Winslow, Arizona. Since they were headed west, George would drive the train with young Roger accompanying him in the engine cab until Winslow. George pulled some strings and arranged for the two of them to ride the rest of the way to Los Angeles in the dormitory car.

George had just given young Roger two model Super Chief F-7 engines that lay in a newly opened box on the boy's lap. The real F-7 engines young Roger and George sat in pulsated loudly.

"Thanks for the engines, Dad!" young Roger said excitedly.

"Least I can do for your birthday," George replied.

The boy sat in the fireman's seat on the left side of the engine cab as views of big sky scenery in New Mexico passed outside. George had asked the fireman if he would mind standing for a while so his son could get the full experience. Roger looked at the gauges and buttons in front of him with wonder. George sat in the other seat, operating the moving train.

Young Roger pointed to a lever. "Dad, can I press that?"

"No. That's the emergency brake. You can pull the horn in a minute." George thought some more and said, "If you're going to be my assistant, you better wear this." George lifted off his red bandana, placed it over young Roger's head, and pulled it down around the boy's neck.

"Dad, why do you love trains?" the boy asked.

"I like to take people on a journey," George answered, "where they can have fun, talk, see the sights, and get to their destination."

"Oh." Young Roger seemed satisfied with the answer.

The train approached a signal tower.

"Roger," George directed, "duck down while we go by here."

Young Roger scooted down, out of sight, and George waved to the tower operator as they passed by the tall building.

"OK," George said when the coast was clear. "You can come up now."

The boy popped back up, excited to have kept their journey a secret.

George increased the engine speed and then instructed his son, "Time to blow the horn. Two long, one short, and then one long. Keep it up until we're over that crossing ahead."

Young Roger pulled the rope handle dangling from the ceiling near his dad. The chime horn almost scared Roger as it sounded its warning right over his head above the cab. George tickled him while his arm was raised, and the boy giggled.

Later, young Roger stuck his head out the side window and enjoyed the wind blowing through his hair. George smirked at him but then turned away with a pained expression, deep in thought. The boy brought his head inside, and the two of them stared straight ahead in silence.

"Roger, we don't have much more time, and I need talk to you."

"About what?"

"There's so much I want to tell you…about all that's happened with your mother…"

"Mom said you might say mean things about her."

George paused at his son's downcast look. "I just want you to know it had nothing to do with you. Maybe someday I can tell you more, when you're ready."

The boy popped his head out the window again, to escape his uncomfortable feelings and feel the cool breeze on his face. As they rounded a curve, Roger could see all eighteen cars and five locomotive units spread out over a third of a mile, gleaming in the setting sun. All the cars had been washed in Albuquerque, and that silvery sight stirred a bit of magic in young Roger's soul, one that would lay dormant for years to come. George glanced over to him and then resumed looking out front. They spent the rest of the ride to Winslow, Arizona in silence. George kept the conversations light for the rest of their trip to Los Angeles in the dormitory car.

Roger returned to the present, still looking at the model train set. He leaned over to look down into the model tunnel. The engine's light shone out of the darkness.

* * *

Later that evening, a lone office light remained lit on the darkened general office floor of Allied Sky Airways as Roger sat in his office, working on his laptop. He looked tired. Paperwork with the Allied Sky Airways logo covered his desk. He stared at his computer work in a vegetative state. He couldn't help but think about what Chapman had said: "You'll continue to live in misery." *Could that have anything to do with why I have such a short fuse with my anger?* he asked himself. *No.*

He pushed the paperwork aside and looked at the computer with renewed energy. He did a Google search for "Railroad Passenger Car Rebuilding." At the top of the list, he found a website that got his attention: "Avalon Rail Inc., Milwaukee, Wisconsin."

After having second thoughts, Roger shook his head, wondering why he'd bothered to look. He powered off his laptop, and the screen went dark.

Suddenly the screen came to life again, startling Roger. It played a continuation of the 1950s film commercial for the Santa Fe Railway Super Chief he'd seen on the airplane. A beautiful young woman appeared in the film, looking at a travel brochure.

The narrator said, "Uh, I beg your pardon, young lady. You're planning a train trip?"

"Yes, I am," the beautiful young woman responded, "to Southern California."

Roger tried pressing different keys on his keyboard but couldn't get the commercial to stop.

"Then you must be planning on travelling on the new Super Chief," the narrator continued.

"Well, not exactly," she said. "Why the new Super Chief? To me, a train is just a train, something you travel on from hither to yon."

"Indeed," the narrator continued. "Then suppose we make a trip from hither to yon, or from Chicago to Los Angeles, and you see for yourself if the new Super Chief is just another train."

"OK by me," she said.

Suddenly Mr. Chapman, waving into the camera with a big smile, replaced her on screen.

"OK," Roger said to Mr. Chapman. "I get it: bring back the Super Chief. I've heard you!"

Roger paced back and forth while Mr. Chapman kept patiently smiling.

"Trust me, Roger," Mr. Chapman said from the computer. "You and others need this."

Roger continued pacing and then stopped and took a deep breath. "OK. I'll think about it."

Mr. Chapman smiled. Then, with no warning, the computer screen went black.

* * *

Roger needed some normalcy back in his life, and a place to release some energy, so he called Brook to schedule a late-night game of tennis at the club in Malibu.

"Only if you're prepared to lose," she said over the phone.

Their game was intense that evening as they both volleyed hard, pounding the ball at each other, venting their frustration with every serve and swing. Roger had been initially attracted to her competitiveness at tennis, but sometimes it turned him off as well—especially when she was so competitive in other parts of her life, always having to have the best and be the best. Roger won the game, though.

* * *

The night of the Allied Sky Airways Christmas Party had arrived. The Fred Harvey Restaurant in Union Station had long since closed, but the separate structure on the Union Station property had kept its name and continued to be rented out for special events.

The room had a warm, nostalgic feel to it. Originally designed by the famous interior designer Mary Colter, the old Fred Harvey Restaurant was where Native American decor met Art Deco. A large Christmas tree stood in the center of the space, and the tile floor was patterned after a Navajo rug. Mary Colter had also designed many of the Santa Fe stations and hotels and may have been influential in the classic interior of the original pre-war Super Chief.

Roger and Brook arrived in a limo at the front of the station. Dressed in formal wear, they exited the limo and approached the historic building. Brook appeared to be in one of her moods, especially after having too much to drink before the night had even begun. She and Roger continued to be at odds about the number of invited guests for the wedding. She poked fun at Roger as they entered the restaurant.

"Maybe your choo-choo friend will show up. He can read us *The Little Engine that Could*," she teased.

Roger ignored the jab.

Later in the evening, Roger and Brook sat at one of the round tables filled with dinner guests. Everyone at the table posed as a friendly blond photographer, who was forty-five but looked thirty-five, took their picture. She caught Roger's eye, not because she had the beauty Brook had that would turn men's heads instantly in a room but because something deep in her eyes and spirit seemed genuine—perhaps a mixture of child-like hope and hidden sadness. He couldn't put his finger on it. Something about her also seemed familiar. He wondered if she was one of those women who become more beautiful as you get to know them. He noticed her walking out of the restaurant to take a break. *Remember: you're engaged,* he thought.

A handsome male guest, Jim, sat next to Brook at the table and kept her attention. Jim had been drinking as much as she had. Roger held his drink and just watched them.

"Ooh, Jim," Brook said flirtatiously, "I'd love to fly on your private jet sometime!"

Under the table, out of Roger's sight, she held Jim's knee tightly.

"You'd always be welcome," Jim said.

"Where do you fly to?" she asked.

"My villa in Italy."

Brook was impressed. Her hand meandered a little further up near his thigh. "A real man of the world," she said. "Roger doesn't have a jet."

"What else doesn't Roger have?"

Jim and Brook laughed. Roger set his napkin aside and left. Brook glanced back at Roger for a second and then resumed flirting with Jim.

Not wanting to play the role of the jealous fiancé, Roger walked out for some air. Tips from his anger management class came in handy again. He'd learned to walk away from certain situations—this was one such situation. *Do I really want a woman who flirts and drinks like Mom did?* he asked himself.

He walked by the south courtyard, filled with flower gardens, into the Union Station north wing ticket area.

Stanchions blocked off the large space, which had been the station's primary ticket office before Amtrak. Now, it stood empty, except for the old moveable ticket counters that were intermittently moved aside for the production of TV commercials and films. The space served as a reminder of the days when train travel dominated the nation's transportation.

Roger gazed at moonbeams glistening through the three huge windows. He ignored the stanchions and walked into the room with wonder, having forgotten how magnificent it was.

The blonde photographer from the party stood in the shadows, taking pictures. Hearing a click, he turned toward her. Her eyes glistened as they made eye contact.

It was magic for an instant as her eyes pierced his soul like he somehow knew her. She smiled and walked around the corner, and Roger looked after her. He started to follow her but stopped. *Remember: you're engaged,* he said to himself again. He then strolled the other way into the lobby/waiting area.

Rows of Mission-style oak and brown leather cushioned chairs connected back to back filled the spacious lobby. Roger looked around, as if for a particular chair. He spotted it, moved to it, and apprehensively sat down. The chair sat in front of a picture window that looked out into the south courtyard. As Roger gazed out the window, more memories flooded his mind.

He flashed back to when he'd sat in this exact same chair in 1971, at the end of his return trip with his dad. Nine-year-old Roger wore the red bandana his dad had just given him and held the box with the model train engines. He looked out the same window then, but it was during the day. He did not look pleased as he watched his parents, George and Marlene, arguing intensely in the courtyard.

Sitting across from him, a pretty forty-seven-year-old woman, Janet, wore a blue dress with a yellow rose on her lapel and a turquoise pendant around her neck. The woman's pretty daughter, seven-year-old Eve sat next to her. They noticed young Roger looking scared.

The lobby doors stood open, allowing the argument between George and Marlene to be heard inside.

"So what if I lied!" Marlene interjected. "I needed a man who can take me places, not keep me stuck out in the middle of nowhere!"

"I gave you everything I had. Why wasn't that enough?" George asked.

"George, you, your life, working for a dying railroad… it's not enough. I've moved on. You need to also."

"I'll move on," George countered, "but you're not taking my son. I'll take you to court."

Marlene stiffened and said, "We'll see about that!"

Tears welled up in young Roger's eyes. He looked away, making eye contact with young Eve—a special moment of calm in the midst of conflict. Her pretty, smiling face was a welcome reprieve from the tension outside.

He started to form a smile as he looked at her, but his smile vanished when Marlene suddenly burst in, followed by George. Marlene picked up young Roger's bag and jerked his hand to rush him out.

"Oh, honey," Marlene said to the boy, "your father is out of control. Let's get out of here."

"Me, out of control?" George said, flabbergasted. "How about all your lying?"

George's raised voice embarrassed young Roger. Loyal to his mother, he willingly let her pull him away across the lobby. George continued to follow them.

"I knew this wasn't a good idea, for you to see him." Marlene said to her son, as she hurried away with him. "He just wanted another chance to be mean to your mother."

Enraged for his mother, young Roger stopped her. He turned around, pulled off the bandana, raised the model-train box, and threw it at George.

This part of the memory was always in slow motion for Roger: the box flew open in midair, and the model engines came out and broke into pieces at George's feet.

George, stricken, called out to young Roger, who was rushing away, "Roger, I'm sorry! I didn't mean to hurt you."

Marlene and young Roger would have continued without stopping, except they ran into Ken—her new husband and young Roger's stepdad. Ken hugged a tearful Marlene and the boy. As they embraced, the boy reluctantly looked back and saw the defeated look on his father's face as he tried to pick up the pieces of the train. Young Roger also noticed young Eve going over to help him. Just then his mother yanked him away again with Ken. It would be the last time he saw his dad.

In the present, Roger sat, amazed at how vividly the memory had remained etched in his mind.

An all-too-familiar voice came from the opposite-facing bench right behind him. "Brings back memories, doesn't it?"

Roger turned, saw Mr. Chapman, and shook his head.

Relying mostly on his cane, Mr. Chapman struggled to rise as he said, "The last time you saw your father."

He limped around to Roger's side and continued. "The Santa Fe Super Chief's last arrival here was on May 2, 1971." Mr. Chapman sat down beside Roger.

"I can't get rid of you," Roger said, irritated. "Are you always this persistent?"

"Only when I have to be. Roger, I need you to make a decision about the train."

"I don't think so," Roger said. "I'm not in as much misery as you say I am."

Knowing better, Mr. Chapman paused a moment and then said, “It hurts.”

“What?”

“That he never came back for you.”

Roger tried to hide his vulnerability but finally blurted out, “I had a lousy father. So what? I moved on. Some things we have to accept in life.”

“You’ve never forgiven him,” Mr. Chapman added gently.

“Why should I? He lost his job, didn’t pay child support, never bothered to see me again…So no, I haven’t forgiven him.”

“What was that you said about not being in misery?” Mr. Chapman asked.

“What of it?”

“A man who can’t forgive is a prisoner in his own cell. Sounds like misery to me. No wonder you can’t sleep and you attend an anger management class.”

The truth of his words stung Roger, and he struggled to hide the tears in his eyes. He pondered, *How did this guy know how to expose my weakness?*

He slumped back in the seat as he realized for the first time that he really was in misery. He had nowhere left to hide. “OK,” he said, admitting defeat. “So maybe you have a point.”

Mr. Chapman perked up, relieved. “Good,” he said. Trying to lighten things up, he added, “I thought I was losing my touch.”

Roger tried to hide a smile. “But I still don’t see how bringing back the Super Chief is going to change anything,”

“Ah, that’s where trust comes in. But time is of the essence. Are you going to do it?”

Roger struggled with the decision. He looked at Mr. Chapman for more answers, but Mr. Chapman just smiled. “OK,” Roger said. “I…I’ll try.”

"Good!" Mr. Chapman responded. "That's a start. And don't forget the list of people I gave you." He saw Brook approaching them from a distance. "My, your fiancée is pretty. But then, you always go for those femme fatales," he said, shaking his head.

"Stay here this time," Roger said.

"A lot of good it will do," Mr. Chapman responded.

Brook, thoroughly exasperated, confronted Roger. "There you are! What are you doing here?"

"Where's Mr. Flyboy?" Roger retorted.

"You're impossible!" Brook countered. "It was just harmless flirting."

Roger dropped the argument and changed the subject. "I've been talking to Mr. Chapman."

He motioned toward Mr. Chapman, but Brook looked at him blank-faced. Mr. Chapman remained in his seat, unseen by her.

"Oh, no," Brook whispered. "You're not going to say you had another visit?" Frustrated and inebriated, she added, "You need to get help." She briskly walked away, a little wobbly.

Roger followed and called, "Brook! Wait!"

Roger turned and gave Mr. Chapman an "any ideas?" look, but Mr. Chapman just shrugged and waved good-bye.

Chapter Four

THE CHALLENGE AHEAD

Why would Roger ever stay with a woman like Brook? For the same reason most people subconsciously stay in destructive relationships: they're attracted to what's familiar. Yes, I would say that's even true of you. Sorry, I don't mean to be harsh—just trying to be honest.

It's easy from the outside to see couples that obviously aren't meant for each other, but when we're emotionally involved in a relationship, we often can't see the forest for the trees. Romantic attraction can do that to people.

I see your point. She was a total flirt and it should have been obvious to Roger. But remember: he didn't see where her hands were under the table.

Regardless, Roger had a lot of other things on his plate…

Several days later Roger's plane landed at Milwaukee's Mitchell International Airport in the afternoon. Waiting in line for a cab, he kept questioning what he'd agreed to with Mr. Chapman. *Just one step at a time,* he told himself as he entered a cab.

After a short ride, Roger exited the cab outside a building far west on Washington Street, behind a cluster of what had once been industrial plants. The sign out front read, "Avalon Rail Inc." He entered the facility and asked a workman where he could find Ms. Crown.

How did a woman like this ever become president of a train factory? Does she ever break the stereotype! Roger thought to himself as he walked through the factory with thirty-five-year-old president April Crown. Polished and fashionable with long dark hair, April sure did break the mold for a railroad shop owner.

As they continued through the area where railroad cars were being refurbished, sparks flew as welders worked on different cars. Roger cut to the chase. "So, what would it cost?"

April pointed to the bottom part of a car in front of them. "Ninety-five percent of the car refurbishing cost is below the floor with truck suspension and wheel rebuilds, new electrical, fresh water, septic, and air brake systems. One could easily spend three hundred fifty thousand dollars and still have never touched the interiors or aesthetics."

"Taking all that into account, what will the total cost per car be?" Roger asked.

"With a car in good condition," she responded, "your total cost will run about one million per car."

Roger let out a sigh. "But if it's not in good condition?"

"That brings us to the second issue: what's the condition of the car from the floor up?"

"OK," Roger said, trying to follow along.

April showed him the siding of a stainless steel car and continued. "Of the Santa Fe cars built in the early 1950s, many were structurally of carbon steel, which was then sheathed with a facade of stainless steel. The two dissimilar metals created significant electrolytic corrosion."

"Which means in English?"

"The carbon steel rotted away," April said, "hidden under the stainless steel exterior fluting. So there is no side sill girder structure. These were built by Pullman Standard and American Car and Foundry. This would require massive metal replacement and add another five hundred thousand to the rebuild cost. Other cars built by the Budd Company didn't suffer the same fate because Budd used all stainless steel, except for the end castings."

"So the goal is to find cars of pure stainless steel?"

"Right," she responded. "By the way, you could save a lot if you refurbished cars owned by a nonprofit rail museum. It could be a big tax write-off.

"Thanks," Roger said.

* * *

Back from his trip, Roger looked effervescent, walking with a spring in his step as he entered a Wells Fargo Bank in Malibu. He didn't quite know why he was feeling so good.

Roger sat across from his financial advisor, who tried to dissuade him from the venture. "Looking at the numbers, I would strongly advise against this."

"Just let me know if it's possible," Roger said.

"Theoretically," the advisor reluctantly continued, "you could swing it if you cash in your inheritance, savings, and stocks; sell your land; and take out a second mortgage. That would clean you out of everything—except the value of your car, and, of course, the income from your job."

Roger looked preoccupied, computing everything in his head. Suddenly he got up to leave, saying over his shoulder, "Thanks."

The financial advisor shook his head as he watched Roger go.

* * *

That evening, Roger met with Brook at La Grande Orange Café in Pasadena. What was once the old adobe-style Santa Fe Pasadena Train Station had since been converted into a restaurant. The old lobby had been beautifully transformed into a dining area with wooden tables and plush booths. A framed picture of the Santa Fe Super Chief Turquoise Room Dinner Menu hung on the wall above Roger and Brook's booth. They were in the midst of an argument.

"Fort Worth, Texas!" Brook said, trying to control herself. "You just got back from Milwaukee!"

"That's where the Burlington Northern Santa Fe Railway is," Roger explained.

"But we have an appointment with the wedding coordinator tomorrow!"

"It will have to be rescheduled," Roger said. "Tomorrow is the only time the president of the railroad can meet."

At an adjoining table, a four-year-old boy, sat with his parents and played with his Thomas the Tank Engine toy. The boy smiled at Roger; Roger smiled back. Brook, in no mood to smile at anyone, ignored the boy.

"Why can't it wait?" she protested. "What happened to focusing on the wedding?"

"I am focused, but there's something more to all this. Mr. Chapman showed me things no one could know. He's right. I've been miserable."

Brook, trying to maintain her composure and patience, shifted agitatedly in the booth.

"If he knows all that," Roger continued, "he must know why I need to bring back this train."

"You don't even know if this guy exists."

"Oh, he exists—you just can't see him."

Brook, about to lose it, shook her head. The boy got off his chair and headed toward them with his toy train.

"Roger, you need help," Brook said pointedly. "I gave you the number for a shrink. Get therapy, get over it, and grow up!" She got up to leave.

"Thanks for your understanding." Roger sighed.

Roger sat there alone for a minute, until the boy from the next table tapped on his arm to show him his toy train.

Roger welcomed him. "Hey, sport. That's a nice engine!" Roger held the blue toy engine in his hands.

* * *

The next day, an older pair of hands held a Lionel detailed O gauge scale model of a Santa Fe F-7 diesel engine. Thomas Peabody, sixty-five years old, was president of the Burlington Northern Santa Fe Railway, which had recently changed its public name to simply BNSF Railway. A good-natured man wearing small, round, wire-rimmed glasses and a three-piece suit, Peabody looked like a classic rail-road executive from yesteryear. He could have been mis-taken for the actor William H. Macy.

He showed off his display to Roger in his office at the BNSF Campus Headquarters in Fort Worth, Texas. Framed posters of trains and original Frederick Remington oil paintings of the West lined the walls. A sign on the door read, "Thomas Peabody, Chairman, President, and CEO."

"They were beautiful engines," he reminisced, setting the engine back on his bookshelf. He turned to Roger. "Let's take a walk."

Roger and Thomas strolled through the courtyard of a group of modern brick and glass office buildings. Four old railroad executive cars on pedestals framed the courtyard.

"I'm sorry, Roger," Thomas said. "This is out of the ques-tion. We are no longer in the passenger business."

"But don't you miss those days?" Roger asked.

"Sure, but I'm missing something else here. You will put up all this money, but the BNSF will still own the cars? Just so you can use the Santa Fe Super Chief name for one trip?"

"I know it sounds crazy, but that's the deal," Roger admitted.

"The engines will cost more than the cars to get in shape," Thomas continued. "I don't think they've gone over twenty miles an hour in fifty years."

"My research shows you have five original Super Chief streamlined cars," Roger said, "which all have some wear and tear on them. Is that correct?"

"Yes."

"I'll need to lease the other four cars from independent owners, including the Pleasure Dome."

"What about the track access fees, insurance, and staffing payroll?" Thomas asked.

"I'll take care of all that."

Thomas began softening to the idea. "And you're ready to give a full personal financial disclosure?"

"Of course," Roger said.

"We will have to approve the crew and food preparation to include items off the original menus. And you will have to have…"

"I know," Roger interrupted. "The French toast."

"You have done your homework." Thomas laughed.

They strolled along another outside courtyard and proceeded into a former California Zephyr Silver Penthouse dome car, renamed Prairie View, on display. Once inside, Roger saw the old dome car had been gutted, leaving just one large open dining area with tables and chairs. The original dome windows were exposed to the first floor, serving as a protruding skylight in the middle of the space. The two men continued their discussion as they sat at one of the tables.

"I'm still not clear why you want to do this," Thomas said. "Why not just rent one of those luxury railroad club trains that tour around the country?"

Roger paused, trying to figure out what to say. "Thomas, are you a spiritual man?"

Thomas appeared a bit uncomfortable and hesitantly said, "Yes."

"Have you ever felt like you were called to do something? And you knew if you didn't, you wouldn't be true to yourself?"

"Sure. We all have dreams."

"I feel called to bring back the Super Chief. Besides, it will give joy to a lot of people to see it brought back to life—if only for just one run. It will also bring great PR to the BNSF."

Thomas laughed and said, "I thought I was a rail fan—but you take the cake!"

"So is it a deal?" Roger asked.

"You actually had me at 'French toast,'" Thomas admitted. "If you have the funding, I think we can work something out."

* * *

Meanwhile, back at the headquarters of Allied Sky Airways in Santa Monica, Jack King came into Dena's office carrying some reports. "Where's Roger?" he asked. "He's not picking up on his cell."

"He's taken two personal days," Dena responded.

"Not a good time," King grumbled, and handed her the reports. "Make sure he looks at these when he gets back."

"I'll put them on his desk."

After King left, Dena walked into Roger's office and set the reports on his desk. She noticed the book *Santa Fe, The*

Chief Way sticking out from under his papers. With growing interest, she began to flip through it. She saw a photo with three Navajo men wearing bright red shirts and dress bands around their foreheads. The inscription below the photo read, "Super Chief Indian Guides Across New Mexico."

Dena's eyes moistened and she became tense as she continued staring at the photo. She abruptly shut the book, collected herself, and strode out of the office.

* * *

Roger used his second personal day to visit the Arizona Railway Museum in Chandler, Arizona, near the Grand Canyon. It was a crisp sunny day with scattered cumulous clouds. He enjoyed breathing in the clean air at the high altitude compared to the smoggy air in the Los Angeles basin.

Roger and the rail museum president, Ned Lord, walked along the rails, past several old streamlined cars sitting along the track. Ned's white hair gave him a distinguished look.

"She's up here just ahead," Ned said. "I could include her with the other two cars."

"I haven't been able to find another Pleasure Dome anywhere," Roger said.

"Only six of them were built."

They walked up and found the Pleasure Dome, bearing Santa Fe number 504. It was in bad disrepair—boards held down a green tarp on the roof that stretched over the broken part of the dome.

Seeing Roger's jaw drop, Ned said, "I told you, she's pretty beat up. Vandals got inside. We've never been able to raise the money to get her refurbished."

They proceeded inside, and Ned turned on his flashlight. The car looked worse from the inside. Water damage and vandalism had destroyed it. They walked up the steps and entered the dome, which was in shambles: broken glass, ripped seats, torn walls, wires and moldy insulation exposed. Roger looked aghast. He didn't know if April Crown would be able to fix something in such bad condition.

As they walked back to the museum office, Roger pondered what he should do. *Should I make a deal with this guy and hope April can perform some magic, or wait and try to hunt down one of the other five Pleasure Domes—if they even still exist?* He decided to give it a try, and they shook hands. The deal wasn't bad, Roger thought, since it included one of the last Super Chief observation cars, Vista Canyon, even though it had lost its beautiful teardrop round end to a squared off look back in the fifties so the railroad could run it midtrain as well as at the train's rear.

* * *

Back at Allied Sky Airways a few days later, Roger attended a meeting in the glassed-in boardroom with the CEO, King, and ten executives.

Noticing that Roger seemed disinterested after King's presentation, the CEO asked, "Roger, where's the razzle-dazzle we're all used to from you? You haven't chimed in."

Roger and King exchanged glances.

"I don't sense you're into this new campaign," the CEO continued. "As I've said before, I want to create an environment in this company where people can freely speak their minds. What do you really think?"

King gave Roger a warning stare.

Roger paused, slowly got up, and went to the front of the conference table. "You want to know what I really think?" he began. "I think we have it all wrong. Because of our own greed, we pack people into planes like they're a can of sardines. And then we give them a tiny bag of peanuts—as if that makes up for it!"

"We're in business to make a profit for our shareholders," King interjected.

"No," Roger continued. "I call it ripping people off. We keep giving the public less and less, while finding ways to charge more and more. What are we going to start doing next? Charging them to use the lavatories?"

King was about to blow his top. "You're out of line!" he said.

"No. Let him continue," the CEO said.

"You want to know what I really think?" Roger continued with passion. "I think we should be about enjoying the journey. We've lost our purpose. We should be about creating an affordable travel experience where people can connect and tell their stories in comfort. Whatever happened to smelling and seeing the countryside? All we do is fly over it. We can't experience a connection with our country from thirty thousand feet up.

"And while I'm on the subject of greed, we've lost our way on how we're treating our own. When we've slashed the pay of our pilots and flight attendants, no wonder so many of them are stressed out. I don't see any of *our* pay being cut. In fact, most of us have gotten bonuses this past year. It's not right. We should be ashamed of ourselves. I for one vote to return my bonus to go toward the flight attendants' pay. How about you?"

The room was silent as everyone's faces turned red. King and the other executives turned toward the CEO, wondering what he was going to do. Roger was on shaky ground.

"Roger," the CEO said, "wait outside as we discuss this matter."

Roger nodded and got up to leave. As he walked toward the door, his cell phone vibrated. Startled, he looked at it:

"April Crown, Avalon Rail Inc." Roger quickly exited to take the call outside the boardroom's glass walls.

"Hi, April."

"Hey, Roger," April said. She got right down to business. "The good news is the five sleepers are pure stainless steel, so there isn't the massive metal replacement, and the Vista Canyon is in very good shape."

Roger noticed some executives in the boardroom looking back at him. He also saw King's angry gestures. He moved out of their sight to continue his phone conversation. "And the bad news?"

"That Pleasure Dome is stainless-sheathed carbon steel, with leakage through the window sash and heavy corrosion. Sorry."

"So I have to come up with another five hundred grand?"

"Yes, approximately. We'll have to speak again when we've taken the fluting off the sides."

Roger rubbed the back of his neck, letting out a sigh. "OK...go ahead."

"I'm also still working on finding you some original Santa Fe F-7 engines," April added. "Those could cost you more than the cars, especially since most were converted to switchers when Santa Fe got out of the passenger business, but I think we can find at least a pair of A units and a B."

Roger's face contorted; he knew this was going to cost him.

King stormed out of the meeting and motioned for Roger to follow him down the hall. Roger nodded. "Gotta go."

Roger sat in front of Jack King's desk while King made out some paperwork. King's office was twice as spacious as Roger's. Roger looked around at the blank walls thinking, *Doesn't this guy have any interests outside this company?*

King finished writing and slipped a piece of paper out from a folder on his desk. He handed it to Roger. "This serves as our official warning to you. If it were my decision,

I would have fired you on the spot. Where do you get off thinking you can talk to us like that?"

Roger didn't respond. He just looked down at the paper, embarrassed, thinking, *What did I just do? What got into me? I can't believe I said those things. You idiot.*

But then two quotes came into his mind to replace his self-loathing. The first was "*And the truth will set you free.*" He'd only spoken the truth. The second was *"Thou doth protest too much."* King had only reacted so harshly because he couldn't handle the truth. A sense of relief soon replaced Roger's inner feelings of embarrassment. It had admittedly been a politically incorrect move for his career, but he had told the honest truth—and that felt liberating. He always loved that old movie, *Network*, where the newscaster, Howard Beale, said, "I'm mad as hell, and I'm not going to take this anymore!" *At least Howard would be proud of me. He'd understand*, he thought.

"Besides today's ludicrous insubordination, your attention has been elsewhere. You've been doing research on railroads on company time. Another infraction, and we will start your termination process. Do you have any response or questions?"

"No, I…I'm sorry? No. I mean, I only used my own personal computer during lunch and after hours."

"No excuses. You're using Allied Sky's Wi-Fi system. I need executives who are interested in planes, not trains."

"Yes, sir." Roger sighed as he got up to leave.

When Roger returned to his office, he felt he needed to get away for a few minutes. He invited his assistant, Dena, to go outside for coffee.

They sat on the edge of a large water fountain in front of an office building, nursing their drinks. Dena was always easy to talk to, and Roger appreciated her loyalty. He sometimes mused what it would be like to be in a relationship with her, but he felt more like a big brother to her and kept clear boundaries in their relationship.

After venting his frustrations and fears over possibly losing his job, he noticed she seemed bothered by something. He knew from previous experience to let her have time to process her thoughts, so he sat quietly, waiting.

"Why did you ask me that time if I knew anything about the Santa Fe Super Chief?" she asked.

"You were on a list of people to invite for the trip."

"What list? What trip?" she asked.

"I'm restoring the Super Chief and organizing a trip from Chicago to Los Angeles."

"Why would you do that?"

"It's a long story, but you were on the list."

"Who gave you the list?"

"It was given anonymously with all expenses paid," Roger said.

Dena paused and reflected for a moment. "I wasn't up front with you," she confessed. "My father worked on the Super Chief. The Santa Fe hired Navajo and Pueblo to be onboard tour guides in New Mexico and Arizona. Maybe that's why I'm on your list." She paused a moment. "Did he put you up to this?"

"No. As I said, it's an anonymous donor. I don't know why you're on the list. I don't even really know why I'm even organizing it."

They sat silently for a few moments.

"Hey, besides getting you to go on the trip," Roger said, "I'm going to need administrative help. Could you…"

Dena abruptly rose to go, becoming tense. "I'm not going on the trip," she said. "And I can't help."

Roger was taken aback, and confused.

"Did I say something?"

She shook her head, holding back tears, and briskly left. Roger looked after her, concerned. Not wanting to cause any more harm, he decided not to try to follow her. *How many people can I tick off in one day?* he asked himself.

she came in
on the
Super Chief
... of course
Santa Fe

Chapter Five

THE LIST

What was with all the beautiful women in Roger's life? Brook, Dena, and then April Crown? He did have his opportunities.

Yes, I can understand how you would want him to end up with someone other than Brook.

Who? I'm not going to answer that yet. Like any storyteller worth his or her weight, I'll let you keep guessing for a while. I have to laugh, because you really don't like going through the journey, do you? Just hang in there with me.

Next I want to tell you about that list…

Roger left work early and got back to his house in Malibu by late afternoon. He spent the drive home thinking about the day's events. He suddenly realized he hadn't called Brook. She was away on a ten-day combined work and leisure trip in Florida. She would be spending the first few days at a real estate convention before hanging out with some girlfriends for the remaining time. *How am I going to tell her what I did?* He decided to wait until he got home to call her.

At his house, he took a shower and sat at the kitchen table, dressed in his bathrobe, staring at his cell phone in front of him thinking, *She'll flip out—I know it. Maybe just wait until she gets back. Anyway, nothing's happened yet. I still have my job. It would just get her upset. Why can't I be more political, like she is with all her realtor friends? She's always telling me I wear my feelings on my sleeve too much. Maybe she's right.* He picked up the phone and called her, but it went to voice mail. "Hey, Babe. Call me when you get a chance…I love you."

Just then, he took out the list Mr. Chapman had given him from his wallet and thought, *I wonder who these people are? Why are they on this list? What's so important for them to go on this train ride? I might as well start calling.*

He began with the first person on the list: Wixie Wilson. Roger would soon learn Wixie was an eight-five-year-old African American gentleman, living at a retirement complex in the Pullman section of Chicago with two other African American men on the list: Curtis Gibson and Henry Wellington. Wixie, a former classic railroad waiter on the Super Chief, was full of charm.

When Roger called, they were all playing shuffleboard. Wixie had his cell phone in one hand and a shuffleboard stick in the other and pushed the disk as he spoke with Roger, who introduced his proposal.

"So, Wixie, are you up for it?"

"The Super Chief!" Wixie responded. "I'm there! Beats all this shuffleboard. I hope my legs can hold up. Haven't served in twenty years! I'll put Curtis and Henry on."

Wixie accidently dropped his phone and shouted to the other men. "Curtis! This gentleman wants you to cook again on the Super Chief!"

Curtis Gibson, former chef on the Super Chief, was in his late seventies. Wixie handed him the phone, and he spoke to Roger in a slow drawl. "You know, on the Super Chief, we used to hire cooks. They couldn't make that French toast. I'd have to show them how to make it. They couldn't make it. You know, Pearl Bailey told me she loved my French toast. I also cooked for Elizabeth Taylor and Richard Burton. Never met them, though. Count me in."

Roger checked off Wixie and Curtis on his list.

Henry Wellington, former porter on the Super Chief, got on the phone next. Henry was charming also, but years of hard work had slowed him down more than the other men. "Depends on whether my arthritis kicks up," he said. "Good Lord willing, I'd like to take one more ride on her."

Roger took that as a yes, ended the call, and made a check on his piece of paper.

Next on his list was Chester Young from Greensboro, Vermont. Sixty-five-year-old Chester wore overalls and held a rake as he stood near his cows in his old red barn, in need of repair, overlooking Caspian Lake. The sun was beginning to set, and he'd been about to call it a day when Roger called his cell phone. He had an obvious loneliness in his voice as he spoke with a thick Vermont accent.

"The Super Chief, you say? Rode it once when I was in high school. Well, I'd have to find someone to milk my cows. It's hard to get anyone these days. No one's interested in farming anymore. Maybe should have sold the place when I had the chance back a long...I don't know. I'll think about it."

Roger placed a question mark on his list next to Chester's name. Continuing down the list, he called Violet Briggs from Beaufort, South Carolina.

Violet, also sixty-five, was having tea and watching a rerun of *Golden Girls* in her quaint living room, decorated with flowered wallpaper and well-placed lace linens on the antique furniture. Raised a Southern belle, Violet exuded Southern charm.

"Why, Mr. Storm, you have such a lovely voice. How could I ever turn such a sweet voice down! My daddy used to take us on the Super Chief. Why that French toast was out of this world! I wouldn't miss this for the life of me!"

Roger checked off Violet's name, leaving only Janet Thompson, from Santa Monica, California, on the list. She lived in the Film Community Retirement Home near Roger's office. He did a Google search and found out she'd starred in quite a few movies during the 1950s.

He spoke to her on the phone for a few moments, but she seemed a bit confused, so he decided to stop by the next morning to try to see her in person.

As he parked his car in the parking lot of the retirement home, he rehearsed what he might say to the receptionist to get past her. He knew a retirement home such as this would be tight on security. It would help his cause that he had learned Janet's room number was 1971 from his conversation with her the night before. Old movie stars often didn't want fans or the paparazzi to see them in their aging condition, preferring to be remembered the way they looked in their glory days.

When a star died in a home like this, it was often kept secret from the tabloids, which was understandable in terms of privacy. But sometimes their families or publicists didn't want the public to know the former star had died in such a lonely condition because they felt it would somehow tarnish their image—as if it made any difference. But such was the way in Hollywood, where image meant everything and the reality of life's hardships was somehow something to be ashamed of and hide.

As he sat in his car outside the nursing home, Roger was reminded of his mother's last years after she was diagnosed with cancer. She, however, was wealthy enough to have in-home hospice care and live in the expensive house Ken had given her until the end. Ken had died of a heart attack in 1990, but he'd left her very comfortable.

Although Marlene was not in the entertainment industry, she had adopted many of the attitudes prevalent in Hollywood. She became more reclusive when her looks began to fade, after years of alcohol and cigarette abuse. Plastic surgery could only go so far. Roger remembered how she didn't want even him to see her unless the lights were dim in the room.

As far as money was concerned, she was always afraid of ending up in poverty. When Roger was growing up, she took every opportunity to remind him of the importance of accumulating wealth. She also taught him how to play the stock market at a young age. In her later years, she became a hoarder, filling the house with a mixture of valuable antiques and junk. Roger reminded her many times that she couldn't take the U-Haul with her to the grave, but she didn't care. Roger occasionally tried to throw things out, but she would go into a tirade whenever he brought the subject up and accuse him of wanting to steal things from her.

One day when he came to visit, she accused him of being too much like his father, George, and said she was concerned he didn't have enough drive to be wealthy. That statement stung—his father was the last person he wanted to be like.

On his final visits, she kept the conversations superficial for the most part. On the last day he saw her before she died in 2008, all she could talk about was how frustrated she was with the judges' voting on *Dancing With The Stars.* He thought it was sad how lonely, bitter, and paranoid she had become. Even though he could see all of her faults, he kept living with the hope of her approval.

After she died, he was surprised to find she'd left him with several million dollars, along with the value of the house. He knew Ken had made good money, but not that much money. Roger never did figure out how she had accumulated so much wealth.

With such memories of his mother and Ken, Roger got out of his car at the Film Community Retirement Home. He opened the back door and got out a bouquet of flowers he had bought for Janet on his way over.

As he entered the nursing facility, he could see the receptionist was preoccupied with a phone call in an office behind the front desk. Since she hadn't noticed him there, and he wanted to avoid any possible complications in getting access to Janet Thompson, he took the opportunity to find the room himself.

As he walked down the hallway, he reflected on how quiet everything seemed—a silent world in the midst of busy Los Angeles. The smell of Lysol permeated the air.

When he came upon room 1971, the door stood open. He stood in the doorway, unnoticed, and observed the space. It consisted of a single bed and dresser on one side and a lounge chair, coffee table, and TV on the other. On one wall, a poster of the Super Chief hung over the bed. B movie posters from the 1950s with the name "Janet Thompson" listed as a secondary credit covered the other walls. Pictures of a beautiful younger Janet Thompson with different famous actors adorned the top of the dresser, along with bottles of pills and a daily pill tray.

Eighty-seven-year-old Janet sat in a wheelchair with her back to Roger, watching *North by Northwest* on her TV—the scene where Cary Grant and Eva Marie Saint flirt over a meal on a railroad dining car.

Roger walked into the room. "Hello, Janet?"

Without looking at him, she waved him off with her left hand, engrossed in the movie.

"Wait. Just a couple more lines…Yes. That's it, Cary."

She turned off the clicker and swung her wheelchair around, surprised to see such a handsome man in front of her. "I never get tired of that scene." She chuckled. "Who are you?"

"Janet! I'm Roger Storm. I spoke with you over the phone yesterday."

"Oh, yes, the Super Chief."

She invited him to join her for the tea she had previously placed on the coffee table. He poured himself a cup and sat in the lounge chair.

Janet liked his demeanor as he explained further what he was proposing and told her about many of the details that had gone into planning the trip. "So, I've raised all the money to make this one trip possible," he concluded.

"You're a man of faith."

"I hadn't thought about it that way," Roger said, "but I guess you could say that."

"Believing in the supernatural—I like that. Goodness knows we all need some kind of hope in life." Roger nodded.

"I haven't gone to church in years. I used to take my daughter when she was young. But I still believe there's something beyond what we can see with our eyes—'seeing the unseen,' as Eugene O'Neill once said."

One of Roger's interests in life was going to the theater, and he could relate well to Janet and her affinity for quoting from plays and films. "*Long Day's Journey Into Night.*"

"Very good, Mr. Storm. I'm impressed. I regret I never got the chance to play the part of Mary."

"Don't get me wrong—I know it's supposed to be America's greatest play—but it was so depressing. Maybe it was too real."

"You're right. It didn't leave one with much hope. Even though O'Neill saw we get glimpses of the life beyond what we see, he felt most of life was about stumbling in the fog—'for no good reason.'"

Roger nodded and said, "Well, I hope this train ride is not a long day's journey into night, but a long day's journey into light!"

She laughed.

"I don't know how to explain it," he said, "but I do think something special is supposed to happen on this train."

She paused and looked wistfully at him as she considered what he'd said. She was also still curious how he'd found her. "Mr. Storm, how did you get my name? Who gave it to you?"

"I'm sorry. I know it sounds strange, but I'm not allowed to say."

Even though that was not the answer she wanted, there was something about this man Janet liked. He seemed so authentic, with rugged good looks. "My daughter, Eve, is all I have left. I wish she could find a good man. Are you taken?"

Roger smiled and was flattered. "I'm engaged."

"Oh, too bad. I think you'd like her. Besides her, there's not much reason to live."

Roger tried to keep things light. "A little adventure would do you good. You'd have nothing to lose to go on this trip."

She laughed at his charm. "When did you say it is?"

"It will leave on April 29, so it gets into Union Station in Los Angeles by May 2."

A pained look crossed Janet's face. She sighed and said to herself, "Forty years."

Roger didn't know what she was referring to. "Forty years?"

"Forty years since the last trip of the Santa Fe Super Chief—arriving in Los Angeles on May 2, 1971. I was on that train."

Roger now realized the significance of the date and couldn't believe he hadn't caught it before. "Oh, yes. Of course! You were?"

"Yes."

"So was I…Anyway, you just need to fly to Chicago and get on board there. Your ticket is on me."

Janet motioned with her hands in the air. "Oh, I'm too old! And I'm sure Eve wouldn't let me. I broke my hip the last time I tried to travel. I'm sorry, Mr. Storm."

"Please, call me Roger."

"Roger, I appreciate the invitation."

"Won't you think about it some more?" he asked.

"If you say so. You are determined."

Roger felt she was hiding something. "Janet, is there anything important that happened to you on the Super Chief? Any reason you can think of why you would be on that list?"

She turned and looked out the window to the pretty garden. Then she turned back and winked at him. "That, I'm not allowed to say…No. Nothing."

In the doorway, Janet's daughter, Eve Jones, had been watching and listening to their conversation for the past minute without their knowledge. Eve was the epitome of classy, cultured sophistication, but with a warm personality.

Roger had his back to her as she took a picture of them with her camera. "You took me on it, Mother—that's something," Eve chimed in.

Janet laughed. "Oh, this is my daughter, Eve. Meet Mr. Storm."

Roger rose from his seat and turned. "Pleased to…"

Magic, as their eyes met again. Roger did a double take, recalling her as the friendly blonde photographer from the Christmas party at Union Station whose unique beauty had left a lasting impression in his mind. Jolted by the recollection, he dropped his teacup. It shattered on the floor.

Eve laughed consolingly and said, "Mother, you have a clumsy visitor."

"Too bad he's engaged. I had him picked out for you," Janet said.

Eve and Roger laughed and blushed at the same time. He tried to explain his clumsiness. "It's just that…it's you, from our Christmas party at Union Station." He knelt to pick up the pieces.

"You remember," she said, impressed.

"How could I forget?"

"I'm flattered." She smiled and then looked at the broken pieces of the cup in his hand. "Here, just give me those."

Roger placed them in her hand, and she looked at them, but her eyes kept returning to Roger. There was an obvious attraction between them. Janet looked pleased as she watched them interact.

"Actually," Eve said, "I might be able to glue these back together."

Roger said his good-byes to Janet after a few minutes, and Eve offered to walk out with him. He asked Eve if she knew anything about Janet's association with the Super Chief, but she didn't have an immediate answer. Roger noticed she seemed deep in thought as they made their way to the parking lot.

"The most I've ever gotten out of her," Eve began, "is that she once met a nice gentleman on the Super Chief, before she met my father."

"That's something. What was his name?"

"I don't know," she said. "My father was not good to her, and even though she was unhappy in the marriage, she was always faithful to him. After my father died, I went on the Super Chief twice with her, in 1970 and 1971. Funny…each time, on the last day of those trips, she wore an old blue dress with a rose pinned on her lapel. I've never seen her wear that dress or a flower any other time."

"Do you know why?"

"I think it had something to do with meeting that man again. They were each to wear a rose, but I understand he never showed up."

"That's it!" Roger said. "That's what this is about! She's going to get hooked up with that man on this trip."

"I don't want to get her hopes up...but you may be on to something."

Roger became visibly excited. "Look, if you will escort your mom, you can be my guest also—all expenses paid."

"If you asked me to have her take any other kind of trip, I wouldn't even consider it. She's obviously too frail."

"But this?" Roger asked.

"It's not so simple. What you're proposing is bringing back the two happiest times I've ever seen her—both on the Super Chief."

"Is that a yes?"

"I'll work on her and give you a call."

"Thanks. It's been a pleasure," Roger said.

"Likewise."

They began by shaking hands, but then they both reached awkwardly to hug each other. When they did embrace, a magnetic comfort made them linger for a slight moment longer than the usual courtesy hug. They both enjoyed it.

Chapter Six

CUTTING TIES

Yes, Janet was a neat old lady. I liked her also. There was something special, though hidden, about her.

Say that again?

I'm glad you're getting into the story. I appreciate the compliment. Many times in today's world, if there're no comic book heroes, vampires, zombies, or bomb sequences, it's hard to keep people's attention.

Where was I? Oh yes. Roger still had some matters to attend to...

Roger had let time slip away from him at the nursing home. Just as he pulled into his office parking space, he realized he was late for a meeting with Jack King. He also forgot he had put his cell phone on silent and looked to see he had missed two calls from his assistant, Dena.

Roger rushed into Dena's office and found her sitting at her desk, a worried look on her face.

"King came and left. He wants you in his office."

Roger let out a sigh and hurried out. Outside King's office, he briskly passed by King's assistant, who nodded for him to enter through the open door. King was working at his desk and looked up as Roger entered.

Before King could get a word out, Roger excitedly said, "I know: I'm late, and the report's not done. Let me beat you to the punch: I quit!"

"That's great. Are you sure?"

"Yes," Roger said with a relieved smile.

"Put it in writing, and you can clean out your desk. I'll have security escort you out."

Roger left, a rebellious lightness in his step. He thought about how quickly King had responded about getting security to escort him out, like he was just itching for him to leave. *Good riddance,* Roger thought.

Roger returned to his office and told Dena the news. Within a few minutes, empty boxes arrived, along with a security guard waiting outside his door, in full view of his every move. Roger wondered, *Why does there have to be such distrust in corporations? What did they think I was going to do? Run off with extra pencils? Smuggle out their top-secret missile-launch plans?*

Roger started filling the boxes with his possessions as Dena, still in shock, stood nearby, concerned. "Are you sure this is what you want?" she asked.

"It was just a matter of time."

Roger's cell phone rang. It was from April Crown at Avalon Rail Inc. He took the call.

April sat in her office, smiling with the news she wanted to share. "Hey, could you use a miracle today?" she said.

"Yeah, now that you mention it."

"I did some digging, and a short-line railroad has two overhauled F-7 engines with the original Santa Fe warbonnet colors on them, and we can get a B unit to go in between and repaint it. That way, you'll have forty-five hundred horsepower, which ought to be sufficient to make the schedule with only nine cars. They're willing to lease them, along with a stainless steel baggage dormitory car for the crew."

Roger's thoughts were elsewhere. He looked at the disappointment in Dena's eyes as he spoke on the phone. "Oh…uh, that's great news, April…Hey I can't talk now. I got to go."

His somber reaction surprised April. She thought he would be ecstatic about all the money she'd saved him. "OK," she said.

Roger hung up. The reality of what he had just done suddenly replaced the momentary rush and relief of quitting his job. He thought, *How fast can I find another job in this economy? What was I thinking?* He started to look concerned and began to breathe heavily as he took down his marketing award from the wall and placed it in a box. He made a couple of trips downstairs to put his belongings in his car. When he came back upstairs and made sure everything was cleared out, Roger gave Dena a big hug.

She liked being in his arms and wondered if he felt the connection also.

Roger wanted her to know how much he appreciated her, so he lingered with an extra-long hug. "Let's stay in touch," he said.

Tears came to her eyes. She nodded and returned to her desk. He left with the guard close behind him.

Roger drove home wondering how he was going to tell Brook about this latest development. He knew she would be disappointed in him, but sometimes he felt frustrated—like he was just a paycheck to her. Even so, he did have compassion for her and how she'd grown up in poverty with an inconsistent mother who had not provided well for her. Brook's mother had relied more heavily on drinking after her father abandoned them, and she was eventually fired from a number of jobs because of her binge drinking. Brook started working after-school jobs at a young age to take care of them, so Roger could understand how she'd developed her perspective. Nevertheless, Roger thought her childhood wounds had made her place way too much importance on money and the status she thought it could provide her. Since she was still away on her trip, he thought he would buy some time and wait until he could tell her in person.

* * *

Because Brook was still not due back for a few days, Roger took the opportunity to jump on a plane to Milwaukee and inspect the progress April was making on the rail cars. When he got to the factory, he was pleased to find lots of activity going on.

April was glad to see him when she spotted him outside her office window. He immediately apologized for his lack of enthusiasm when she had previously called with the good news about the engines. He explained the circumstances, and she was very understanding. She did wonder, though, how he was going to pay for all this without a job. Regardless of her doubts, she escorted him into her office and brought him up to date on the progress they were making.

After they finished catching up, she proceeded to get back to work by taking out a pane of glass from a box on the floor. Roger felt awkward as he stood across from her with nothing to do and no job to go back home to.

"The Pleasure Dome windows just came in," she said. "They had to be specially ordered."

"I've got time on my hands. Could you use any help?" Roger asked.

"You're not serious? All I have is grunt work."

"Hey, grunt is OK."

She nodded, and Roger proceeded to go change into some overalls he'd brought along.

He helped out with a number of chores. The crew was busy: two electricians tested a generator on the outside of one of the streamliner cars while two carpenters nearby used a table saw to cut paneling.

Roger took it upon himself to provide food and snacks for the crew. After visiting a local grocery store and Starbucks, he made coffee and sandwiches for everyone. April and her employees appreciated his efforts. As they all took a break together, April joked, "You're going to make me look bad, Roger. They're going to expect a full-time catering service from now on."

Everyone laughed.

Later that night, still at the factory, Roger was polishing the stainless steel sleeping car's side exterior by himself. The rest of the workers had gone home, except for April, who was still in her office doing paperwork.

She came out of the office with a somber look and approached Roger. "I've got some bad news: with all the overtime, I project we're going to run over a hundred thousand dollars."

"A hundred thousand?"

"We keep finding more problems with the Pleasure Dome," April said.

Roger dropped his towel and began pacing, shaking his head. April waited for his response. "I don't know what to tell you. I'll have to get back to you tomorrow."

"OK. Just sleep on it and let me know. Sorry to be the bearer of bad news."

"It's OK. It's not your fault. I know you're doing the best you can."

Roger felt compelled to use his excess nervous energy by working into the night, so April gave him a key to lock up before she left. After she exited, he picked up his polishing towel and threw it angrily against the car. He sat down and put his head in his hands.

Suddenly, he heard someone whistling *Working on the Railroad.* He looked under the car and saw a pair of legs on the other side. He walked around and found jovial Mr. Chapman dressed in his porter's outfit, polishing the other side of the car.

"You've come too far to quit now," Mr. Chapman said.

"I have nothing left!"

Mr. Chapman took his time before responding and refolded his towel. "That sure is an expensive wedding you're planning."

"What?" Roger did a double take. *This guy is controlling too much of my life,* he thought. "If I cut out the lobster or limit the guest list, Brook will have a fit."

"What's more important: bringing back this train and reconciling relationships, or buying a luxury you don't need, with money you don't have, to impress people you don't even like?"

"What does this train have to do with reconciling relationships?" Roger asked.

"You'll know—all in good time. Let's keep polishing."

Mr. Chapman threw Roger another towel and resumed his work. Roger held the towel and shook his head but then decided to continue polishing also. As they worked side by side, Mr. Chapman started humming again. Roger looked at his reflection in the polished stainless steel as he pondered his options and thought of more questions to ask Mr. Chapman. He came out of his trance when he noticed it had become quiet. He looked up. He should have expected it: Mr. Chapman was gone.

* * *

The sun was beginning to set over the Pacific Ocean in Malibu as Brook waited in her car in Roger's driveway for his return from Milwaukee. She looked at her reflection as she primped in the car mirror. She hadn't offered to pick him up at LAX because it conflicted with her salon appointment. Besides, she also didn't feel like going out of her way since he had become so distant lately. He wasn't even around to meet her at LAX when she got back from her trip. As her girlfriends had suggested on her minivacation, she thought Roger needed to prove his interest in her more. Other men, like the independently wealthy Jim she'd met at the Christmas party, were showing her more attention than Roger was.

A beat-up airport shuttle van pulled up the driveway and Roger exited, surprising Brook. The driver pulled out Roger's luggage from the back, and Roger tipped him and thanked him.

After the van sped away, Brook got out of her car and waited for Roger to approach. As he walked toward her, he noticed the quizzical look on her face.

"Why didn't you take a limo?"

"I need to talk to you."

She agreed they would talk after he went into his room to take a shower. She waited in the living room, wondering if she should tell him she had been out to dinner with Jim twice. She decided she didn't have to, since they weren't married yet. And besides, she felt she needed to keep other options open in case things didn't work out with Roger. She believed she had to look out for herself, because no one else would. *All's fair in love and war,* she thought.

Feelings of insecurity replaced feelings of disloyalty as she speculated about what was so important that they needed to have a special talk. She started wondering what he had done now, or if he had met someone new. Becoming anxious, she pulled out a full bottle of scotch along with two glasses and set them on the coffee table. She poured herself a glass and started to drink.

Roger came from his bedroom carrying a pad of paper with calculations written on it. Since it had become dark outside, he brought her over to the dining room table and turned on the lights. She set the scotch and two glasses on the table, and they sat down.

"I quit my job."

"You *what?*"

"I had to."

"Why?"

"I was living a lie. I need to focus on this train."

"And now what?"

"We need to cut the costs of the wedding."

The full bottle of scotch became half empty within a few minutes. Needless to say, Roger's news of unemployment did not sit well. She tried to remain calm and just listened as he spoke. Then he showed her the calculations for the wedding reception and the costs of rebuilding the train. She poured another glass of scotch and took an added gulp. Her world was crumbling.

"You know how to break a woman's heart."

"It just means having chicken instead of lobster and keeping the guest list down to three hundred."

She got up to circle the table. The liquor had gone to her head, and she kept filling her glass. Roger got up to try to console her, but her body language made him step back.

"My dad was an unemployed dreamer," she said. "He kept waiting for his big break in Hollywood. Left us high and dry. And now here I am, engaged to an unemployed dreamer."

"That's not fair. It's not the same."

"Sure it is. You're going to throw all your money away on this."

"There's more to life than money, Brook…it's not going to make you happy."

"Well, I've been without it, and that was no great shakes."

Roger paused and said, "I'm sorry. I have to do this."

She picked up her purse to leave. "Then you'll have to do it without me. The engagement's off. I have to consider my other options."

"Other options?"

"A private jet to Italy beats taking an old train to nowhere."

Roger felt stung, but he held his anger. She stumbled on her high heels as she made her way out the door. He soon followed her and wouldn't let her drive. Instead, he drove Brook in her car back to her condo on Pacific Coast Highway.

During the drive, he didn't try to talk to her. He could see she was still angry. He glanced over at her as she sat in the passenger's seat with her head turned away from him, looking out the window. The thought he had been trying to repress for the past few months came bubbling to the surface again: even though she was physically gorgeous and he had never experienced such intense physical chemistry with a woman, her lack of inner beauty did not match her outer beauty. He also thought how odd it was that when people break up, everything reverts to silence—as if the two people never knew each other.

He pulled the car up in front of her place and turned off the engine. She turned suddenly and yanked the key out of the ignition, and they both got out. She hit the lock button on her key and ignored him as she headed unsteadily toward her door. He looked after her to make sure she got inside OK and then called a taxi to take him back to his place.

Chapter Seven

FINISHING TOUCHES

You saw the breakup of Roger and Brook coming. OK. Fair enough. But, as I said, it's always easier to see things when you're not emotionally involved.

Roger still had some loose ends to attend to...

Roger had a hard time getting used to being unemployed. He tried to use his time wisely by spending the first few weeks doing job searches on his computer. No responses. He also made time to jog more often. Even though he had fears about his future employment, he at least felt somewhat relieved about his breakup with Brook.

Then the dreaded morning finally arrived: Roger sat on his porch—unshaven, wearing his bathrobe, and sitting in a rocking chair. This wouldn't have appeared abnormal, except it was pouring rain and both he and the chair he was rocking in were getting drenched. He was watching as his cherished blue convertible BMW was raised onto a tow truck in his driveway. The driver from the dealership raised the car slowly, as if to taunt him.

Roger was surprised at how sad he was to lose his car. Even though he disliked the superficiality and materialism he saw everyday in Los Angeles, here he was, going through symptoms of BMW withdrawal. *It's just a piece of metal,* he reminded himself.

The tow truck pulled out of the driveway with his car.

"Ford, here I come," Roger muttered to himself.

He held a wooden train whistle in his hand that he had found on his porch—obviously another present from Mr. Chapman. It was the same kind of whistle he'd had as a child. Blowing it reminded him of another childhood memory.

It was 1972, a year after he'd last seen his dad. Then ten years old, he sat by himself in a rocking chair on the front porch of Ken's house in Pasadena. Marlene came out of the Craftsman-style home with a glass of scotch and a buzz. He kept rocking, looking down the street.

"Honey, your Dad's not gonna come," Marlene said.

"But he's never missed my birthday."

"Well, he's missing this one. Get used to it, honey."

"Is he mad at me for throwing the train at him?"

Marlene knelt by his rocking chair and stopped his rocking. "It doesn't matter. Who loves you the most?"

"Mom," young Roger said.

"And I'm sure you want to make Mom happy." She gave a glaring stare and nodded, inducing him to nod. "So no more talk of Dad. We're gonna go inside now and celebrate your birthday."

"Yes, Mom."

"Let's get rid of that stupid train whistle and find out what new toys Ken has bought you." She took the whistle and threw it aside as they went back inside the house.

The memory of 1972 evaporated as Roger's teakettle whistled from his kitchen. He went in out of the rain, still holding the wet wooden train whistle, and walked into the kitchen to turn it off.

He then walked toward the entranceway to take off his wet robe, but he passed in front of a wall mirror and stopped. He looked dejectedly at himself in his soaked bathrobe and thought, *I look like I've aged ten years in just a few weeks.*

The phone rang, breaking him from this depressing thought. It was Dena. She asked him to meet her the next day in downtown Los Angeles at Philippe's restaurant on Alameda Street.

* * *

In his years living in the Los Angeles area, Roger had vaguely heard of Philippe's but had never been there. It happened to be just up the street from Union Station, on the edge of Chinatown.

After he parked in his "new" used Ford across the street, he carried his briefcase up to an old building with a sign that read, "Philippe, The Original French Dip Sandwiches." This artifact of LA history was established in 1908. When Roger entered, he noticed sawdust chips spread over the floor and train memorabilia covering the walls. While waiting for Dena, he walked to the rear dining room and was captivated by the model trains on display in glass cases. A model Santa Fe Lionel F-7 engine caught his eye.

Dena entered soon after and spotted Roger across the room. She approached him unnoticed as he continued looking at all the historic train information on display.

"I thought you might like this place, with its train theme."

"Dena!" He gave her a big hug.

She felt like asking why he hadn't called her, but she didn't.

"Yes, I can't believe I've never been here. Thanks for letting me know about it." *Boy, is she pretty, but there's too much of an age difference,* he thought.

"Sure. We need to get in line at the counter to order."

After they came back with their French dip sandwiches, tapioca, and the best nine-cent cup of coffee in the city, they chose a quiet booth near the train display. He began thinking, *I wonder why she called to get together here. Is it just to catch up, or is she willing to help with the train project?* In any event, he was glad to see her.

She finally confided in him. "Roger, I didn't let on earlier…My father and I haven't spoken in five years, since I left the res."

"He didn't want you to leave?"

Dena shook her head. "The train reminds me of him, but if you still want help, I'm in."

"You sure?"

She nodded. "Someone's got to keep you organized."

"And you'll come on the trip?"

"Let's not push it," she joked. "Yes, I'll come."

"Good!" He took some papers out of his briefcase. "I'll need your help with booking passengers, advertising, and getting the legal clearances from Amtrak."

"All the things you're not good at."

"Exactly."

They smiled and made extended eye contact, but then Roger looked away and thought, *Don't give her the wrong idea. Keep it platonic. With romance, remember: if you doubt, don't.*

Dena agreed to accompany Roger to the Amtrak offices in Union Station. He felt that with her administrative abilities, he could be sure to cover all the bases regarding insurance and track fees.

They met with the general superintendent of Amtrak's Southwest division, Mr. John Harriman, in a rather small office on the third floor. Harriman got a kick out of their plans and couldn't contain his excitement about Roger's venture as he handed them a stack of papers.

Roger kept thinking, *Harriman, Harriman...That name sounds familiar...Mr. E.H. Harriman of the Union Pacific Railroad, made famous in the movie* Butch Cassidy and the Sundance Kid, *when he sent a posse after the famous outlaws!*

"You don't happen to be related to the famous E.H. Harriman, of the Union Pacific Railroad, do you?"

John blushed and smiled that someone would pick up on his name. He enjoyed the flattery of possibly being connected to a historic railroad tycoon from the early twentieth century. "No. I've been asked that before, but no relation. I wish I had been, though!"

Roger's apparent knowledge of railroad history made John feel even more of a camaraderie with him, so he did his best to help with the red tape with all the paperwork by having his assistant, Lilly Cohan, obtain and complete many of the forms for them.

After they had taken care of all the formalities, Harriman escorted them out of his office. Roger and Dena awkwardly shook hands with him as they tried to juggle all the paper work he had given them.

Harriman called after them, "The Santa Fe Super Chief! Wow! Sign me up!"

* * *

Dena spent quite a few evenings and weekends helping with advertising, website development, and reservations. She saw that her crush on Roger wasn't mutual. He always treated her like a true gentleman, but he never made a move on her like so many other guys did. He had many opportunities when they worked alone together, but he never went there.

He didn't want to jeopardize their friendship and the platonic feelings he had for her—like she was his little sister. He kept reminding himself, *Don't take advantage of her just because you're lonely and it would be convenient.*

Besides, he kept thinking of another woman who mesmerized him—Eve. He called her twice about the trip, but she never called back. She only sent an e-mail stating that she would try to make it with her mother but couldn't promise anything. She concluded she would have to wait until it was closer to the day of departure to see how her mother's health was.

Roger wondered, *Why did she just send an e-mail? I thought she would have at least wanted to talk. Was the electricity I felt just with me? No. She looked at me like there was something more between us. And that hug…I melted in her arms. She must be with someone…but her mother said she didn't have anyone. But how could someone that lovely not be attached?*

One Saturday when Dena was working at his kitchen table, Roger came in from getting the mail, holding up an issue of *Trains* magazine. He opened it up to a full-page advertisement of the trip. A beautiful print from an old painting of the Super Chief covered the page.

The ad read, "The Trip of a Lifetime: The Return of The Original Santa Fe Super Chief. 'The Train of the Stars.' Leaving Chicago, April 29; Arriving in Los Angeles, May 2. With a special stopover in Santa Fe, New Mexico. Passengers are encouraged to wear vintage clothing. Order tickets online at www.returnofthesuperchief.com."

Roger and Dena looked at it with a sense of accomplishment and excitement. Dena surprised him by proceeding to pull out a copy of the *Los Angeles Times.* She went to the Arts and Entertainment section and showed him a full-page color spread of the same advertisement. She also showed him a copy of the *Chicago Tribune* and *The Wall Street Journal,* each with smaller versions of the same ad.

Roger gave her a high-five and a glowing smile.

Chapter Eight

THE DEPARTURE

Are you still with me?

Oh, I'll get to what happened on the train ride.

Yes, it was curious why Roger got the silent treatment from Eve.

Chapman? I'm sure some people would agree with you that he seemed a bit odd. As far as whether he was a ghost or an angel—hold your horses. I'll get to all that. I just wanted to make sure you were still with me. Now where was I? Oh, yes…

The big day was drawing near. Roger flew out to Chicago a few days early, on April 26, to make all the final preparations. Dena decided to meet him at Chicago's Union Station on April 29 at eight a.m., a couple of hours before they were scheduled to depart.

On April 27, he decided to go to the Amtrak coach yard wash rack down at Sixteenth Street and the Chicago River to see the train being washed for final preparations. He stood anxiously by the side of the track in front of where the train would soon pass through the spray. A few minutes later, he saw the train inch toward him at the required two and a half miles per hour for the washer. Its beauty and power mesmerized him, and a chill went up his spine.

Bearing its well-known red, yellow, black, and silver warbonnet design, the famed Santa Fe engines forged through the jet-spraying train-washing machine, pulling the stainless steel cars behind. The Super Chief was now almost ready.

Roger stayed at The Palmer House, about a half-mile from Chicago's Union Station. He couldn't sleep the night before the big day. Thoughts kept churning in his head. He had made several calls to Eve over the past week but still hadn't heard anything back from her. *Will she bring Janet?* he wondered. *If she doesn't, what will that do to the trip?* Roger hadn't heard anything more from Mr. Chapman either. All he knew now was that he needed to show a further step of faith by just going forward, one day at a time.

The big day finally arrived. Wearing a classic gray flannel suit with white handkerchief and pulling a suitcase, Roger started off for an early morning walk that would end at Union Station, Chicago. He thought the walk might relax him.

He couldn't believe he had sat up the night before reading a book about the history of the Santa Fe Super Chief. He wondered, *Am I turning into one of those crazy rail fans?* He found himself fascinated with the discovery of such things as how the Super Chief had originally left from Dearborn Station in Chicago, not from Union Station, which was now the lone inter-city railway station left in the city.

But Roger also found himself feeling inexplicably saddened when he read about how rapidly railroads had lost their popularity, as evidenced in Chicago: Dearborn Station, once serving six railroads itself, was one of six major Chicago railroad stations until the early 1970s, when Amtrak consolidated most of the different railroads, eventually closing all their remaining stations except Union Station. Even though he was disappointed to learn the train shed and tracks of Dearborn Station were torn up, Roger was relieved to hear that the old station building, at the symbolic head of the modern day Santa Fe Trail, had been saved and turned into an office complex in the 1980s.

Roger decided to take the half-mile-long diversion over to the old location of Dearborn Station—partly out of curiosity to see what it now looked like and partly to pay a fitting homage to it on the day the Super Chief would return.

Sure enough, he found the Romanesque Revival brick building with clock tower still there. The train shed had been turned into a community park. As he looked at the clock tower, a special orange glow of early morning sunlight hit the brick facade. Roger couldn't help but think it was a symbol of its former heyday being displayed on this special day.

Continuing on his way to Union Station, he kept asking himself the questions that continued to haunt him and wondering how the day would play itself out. *Will Eve and Janet show up? What about all the other passengers on the list? What about Mr. Chapman? Am I crazy for doing this? Yes. Yes, I am.*

He eventually entered the Great Hall at Union Station, Chicago, where morning shafts of light shined through the tall windows of the Beaux Arts-style lobby. He encountered a crowd of rail fans, spectators, and passengers, some dressed in modern and some in period dress. Several modern-day film stars also made an appearance for the train ride.

A female TV reporter with cameraman spotted Roger and took him aside for an interview. Roger tried to look confident to cover his nervousness. The reporter looked into the camera and said, "Who would believe bringing back an old train would cause this much excitement? Chicago hasn't seen this many celebrities turn out since the *Oprah* finale. We have the man responsible for bringing back this once-famous train, the Santa Fe Super Chief, often referred to as 'The Train of the Stars.' His name is Roger Storm. Mr. Storm, why have you gone to all this trouble and expense for one trip?"

Back in Los Angeles, Brook watched the interview on TV as she ate breakfast in her condo. Her eyes lit up when she saw Roger on the screen. She turned up the volume, suddenly impressed with the coverage.

"To help people relive a treasure from our past," Roger answered, "and make us remember who we were. I'm hoping this is one special ride for everyone on board."

"Is it true that some tickets are going for ten thousand dollars apiece?"

"That would be for a double drawing room that can sleep four people. Most tickets are half that amount for two people. In other words, it comes out to twenty-five hundred per person," Roger explained.

"One expensive ride to be sure," the reporter commented. "Thank you, Mr. Storm."

Roger nodded and left.

The reporter turned her attention back to the camera and said, "There you have it—a piece of Americana being brought back to life. It makes you wonder if some of those old movie stars—Humphrey Bogart, Gary Cooper, Cary Grant, Marilyn Monroe, or Grace Kelly—will come back to life and want to get back on. If they do, we'll be sure to let you know, so stay tuned."

On the train platform, out of sight to passengers in the station, the bright red nose of the warbonneted diesel locomotive stood facing Los Angeles, some 2,222 miles west. Behind it, the majestic line of stainless steel cars awaited its passengers, the train having been backed into the station much sooner than most trains would have been. The light reflecting off the newly polished cars gave the train a grand mystique. The red-carpeted platform stood empty except for the porters putting a final shine on the handrails at each doorway before standing formally at attention at the car entrances. The conductor and assistant conductor completed some paperwork and prepared to man the check-in counter at the entrance to the platforms.

It was a proud moment that Roger couldn't fully appreciate as he paced expectantly, checking his watch near the Vista Canyon observation at the rear of the train, on whose windowed face sat an illuminated sign bearing the words, "Santa Fe Super Chief" with an Indian chief motif.

Dena stood next to Roger, and handed him some papers from her clipboard. "Here's a hard copy of the final passenger list—fully booked."

Roger took the papers and kept pacing.

"What's with the pacing?" she asked.

"This whole thing is crazy."

"It will be OK."

Up ahead, outside the dining car, Wixie Wilson and Curtis Gibson were quietly joking around.

"Curtis, you sure you remember those recipes? I don't want to have to return food to the kitchen."

"Listen to you!" Curtis responded. "I'm just afraid the food ain't gonna get there. Maybe we should get you a wheelchair!"

"Wheelchair! Just as soon as we get you a kitchen nurse to be on standby," Wixie replied.

"That nurse would be looking after you, not me," Curtis said. They both laughed.

Porter Henry Wellington shuffled over toward them from the sleeping car doorway and said, "Hey, what you two jabbering about?"

"We're worried you're gonna fall asleep when you make up those beds," Wixie said. "Someone's gonna come back to their room and find you snoring in their bed."

"Least I don't snore as loud as you do," Henry said to Wixie. "No one's gonna get any sleep in the dormitory car with you in there." They all laughed and then quieted down. They readied themselves by adjusting their uniforms, and then paused to appreciate the moment.

"Feels good to be back. Don't it brothers?" Henry said.

"Yes, sir. Sure does," Wixie said.

"Just like the old days," Curtis said.

They were interrupted by a classic public address announcer's voice from yesteryear over the sound system: "May I have your attention please? Passengers may now board at Track S Twenty-Eight, Santa Fe Railway Train Seventeen, the Super Chief." Wixie and Curtis jumped back on the dining car and Henry hurried back to the sleeping car doorway and stood at attention.

The lobby doors at the end of the platform burst open, and the crowd of passengers excitedly walked up to get on board.

The public address announcer continued, "The Atchison Topeka and Santa Fe's first-class, all-sleeping-car train to Los Angeles, making stops only in Kansas City, Dodge City, La Junta, Raton, Lamy, Albuquerque, Gallup, Winslow, Flagstaff, Needles, Barstow, San Bernardino, and Union Station, Los Angeles. *All aboard!*"

Among the various passengers heading up the ramp were the invited guests on Roger's list. Violet Briggs from South Carolina had a redcap porter wheel her luggage behind her. She looked back and winked at him. "I just love men in uniforms!"

The redcap porter smiled.

A few yards away, Chester Young from Vermont carried his suitcase. He wore a plaid shirt and dress pants, which was very unusual for him. He couldn't remember the last time it wasn't a Sunday when he wasn't wearing overalls.

A few railroad officials were also on hand for the trip. BNSF president, Thomas Peabody, carrying a briefcase, walked ahead of three BNSF executives and two Amtrak executives. They all wore suits. Another redcap porter pushed a large cart behind them with their luggage.

When they came upon the train, the executives marveled at the sparkling cars.

"The consist looks great! It's all uniform," one of the Amtrak executives said.

"Reminds me of the old days!" a BNSF executive chimed in.

Roger saw the executives approach and greeted Thomas, shaking his hand. Dena stood nearby, holding a clipboard.

"Welcome!" Roger said.

"She looks like new!" Thomas said. "Very impressive. As good as our own executive train."

"Thanks for your help."

"Don't mention it," Thomas said. "Everything's set. I've got the awards with me."

"Great!"

After the executives boarded the train, two out-of-shape rail fans wearing train insignia T-shirts accosted Roger.

"Mr. Storm, where did you ever get those F-7 engines?" the first asked.

Roger, caught off guard, said, "They were loaned to us."

"Did you know the F-7s were built between 1949 and 1953, and have fifteen hundred horsepower?" the second fan added.

"No. I did not know that."

"But you have a Phase One engine," interjected the first rail fan.

"No. It's a Phase Two. It has the vertical upper grille," the second fan protested.

"No. It's a Phase One!"

Seeing that the argument was getting heated, Roger excused himself. "Nice to meet both of you." He rolled his eyes and walked away while the two rail fans kept debating.

"Phase Two!"

"Phase One!"

Meanwhile, inside Chester Young's bedroom in the Super Chief sleeping car, Chester unpacked his suitcase, his door standing open. Each climate-controlled bedroom came with an enclosed private toilet and sink, large picture window, cushioned arm chair, couch, vanity mirror, small closet, optional folding table, shoe shine compartment, porter buzzer, and fan.

In the evening, the porter would turn the couch into a made-up lower berth, and if the bedroom was occupied by two passengers, he could pull down a second berth from the ceiling with ladder. The porter would make up each berth with two crisp sheets, a pillow, and two warm woolen blankets.

At night, a passenger put their shoes in the shoe locker and in the morning, they would turn up freshly shined, and with a newspaper from the last major city.

In the corridor outside Chester Young's bedroom, porter Henry Wellington carried Violet Briggs's suitcases and passed Chester's room with Violet following.

"We'll be leaving the station in a few minutes, folks," Henry called out. Then he asked Violet, "Where are you from, Ms. Briggs?"

"Beaufort, South Carolina—the most charming place in the world. And call me Violet."

Chester froze in his room at the sound of that voice. He had heard it before.

"Did you ride the Super Chief in the old days?" Henry continued.

"My daddy took me when I was a teenager. He worked for the Atlantic Coast Line."

Chester popped his head out of his room into the corridor and looked at Violet, who was still in the hallway waiting for Henry to finish putting her bags in the next room. She noticed Chester peeping his head out the door.

"Violet? Violet Briggs?" Chester asked.

She looked at Chester and vaguely remembered his features. "That strange accent...Chester, the farmer from Vermont?"

"Yes!"

"I do declare! Chester Young! What are you doing here?"

"Got a call from Roger Storm," Chester responded.

"Me too! Why, I do declare!"

Chester approached her and gave her a big hug. She was attracted by the brute strength of his muscles and found herself a bit flustered when he let her go.

"Are...are you by yourself?" Violet inquired.

"Yup. The Mrs. died about ten years ago. Been pretty lonely on the farm ever since."

"I'm so sorry. That's about how long ago my husband passed. He looked fine, but then one day he died after eating barbecue."

The porter left. Violet stood in the hallway, hesitating. She finally looked at Chester, who looked nervous.

"Well, I'll catch you later, Violet," Chester stammered.

"Not too much later, I hope," Violet said with a thoughtful smile.

Chester returned her smile, and then she went into her compartment first. Chester watched until she closed her door and then entered his room.

On the train platform at the sleeping car entrance, Roger paced and looked at the clock near the platform entranceway: 10:10. No one else was headed toward the train. In the foreground, Roger observed the conductor looking at his pocket watch.

Dena popped her head out of the train stairwell.

"Is someone missing?"

"Just three," Roger said as he kept pacing.

Dena waited by the car near Roger.

* * *

The last few days had been difficult for Eve. She felt torn with what to do about the trip for several reasons.

First, she was flustered by her deep attraction toward Roger and thought maybe she should stay away. *What are you thinking? Even if he were interested, he's engaged. You don't want to get in the middle of that,* she thought.

And she wanted to make her relationship with Peter work. They had been together for five years but never married. She was still trying to get over his affair with his office assistant. He promised he would never do it again, but she knew, if she was honest with herself, that it felt like they were going through the motions. She wanted to trust him, but he had too many opportunities to lie to her. He was always working. And now she had this attraction for Roger, but she didn't want to do to Peter as he had done to her. The pain was too much.

Roger had called several times, but she didn't think she could trust herself if she started communicating with him. Her strong sense of loyalty was sometimes her own undoing—when it meant being loyal to the wrong type of person. She also didn't like change in her life. She was a creature of habit.

Still, she couldn't get Roger out of her head. Why did she feel like she knew him—like he was somehow part of her? Was it mystical? She knew she'd been communicating an interest to him when she lingered in their hug, but she didn't want to open up anything further. It also wouldn't be fair to Roger. So no, she was determined not to return his phone calls. If she were going to go on the trip, she would find a less personal way to communicate.

And then there was Janet's health. She seemed to be getting weaker over the past couple of months. Something in Eve's spirit knew her mother was not going to be around much longer. Should she risk expending her mother's last amount of energy on this trip, or play it safe and maybe have her mother live a few months more by staying put?

Her mother had become like a little child in some ways, and their roles had fully reversed over the past few years. Her mother's eyes glistened with anticipation like a child when they spoke about the trip, much like her own eyes glistened when she was young and promised she could go with Janet on the Super Chief. Her mother had always come through for her, even when it was inconvenient. And now she was in a similar position. To do what was convenient, or to do what was inconvenient?

The third complication was that Peter did not like trains. It would be helpful if he came along to help with Janet, but then she didn't want to deal with his impatience on the train. She had taken him on a cross-country trip by train before, and he did nothing but complain about what a waste of time it was. So she wanted him to come in one way, but not in another. Plus, she felt guilty for thinking it, but she knew if he came, she would not get a chance to get to know Roger.

One part of the decision was settled for her when Peter opted out of the trip after she had invited him. As usual, he said he had too much work to do.

When the time drew near, Eve became more nervous about missing this opportunity. She finally e-mailed Roger's assistant Dena that she would come. She thought that was safer than contacting Roger directly—keep it purely about Janet and not communicate anything otherwise to Roger.

On the night they were supposed to leave from LAX, Eve thought they would have plenty of time since the plane was to arrive in Chicago at six a.m. and the Super Chief wasn't schedule to leave until 10:10 a.m. She would have left a day earlier and stayed at a hotel in Chicago, but she knew Janet had a hard time sleeping in a new bed; so she decided to take the red eye.

To prepare for the event, Eve had bought Janet and her a few classic, 1950s-style dresses. Since they would not have time to change before boarding the train in the morning, they wore their outfits on the plane.

Eve was sweating bullets when a mechanical failure occurred on their plane while they sat on the tarmac at LAX. They had to go back to the gate, deplane, and wait for another plane to take them.

Eve and Janet arrived at O'Hare Airport the next morning at eight thirty a.m., waited for their baggage, and rushed to take a cab. She tried to call Roger on his cell to tell him they were late, but he wasn't picking up. The cabdriver did the best he could to make time on the packed Kennedy Expressway into downtown Chicago.

They exited the cab at the front entrance of Union Station, Chicago, and a redcap porter helped them with their luggage and found a wheelchair for Janet. They went through the front doors into the large lobby. Eve looked at the station clock: 10:10. The redcap porter did not have a radio and said they had to hurry.

* * *

As Roger continued pacing, he kept wondering why Eve hadn't returned his calls and had only communicated recently by e-mail to Dena. He could tell Eve was keeping things at a distance. He had learned that when a woman responds to a phone call by e-mailing back, she was not interested. He could normally accept that, but he knew in this case there was something more between them. He knew when a woman showed interest in him—and he kept thinking she was showing interest in that hug. *But was I wrong? Did I somehow misinterpret it? Did she think of it as strictly platonic? What does it matter anyway? A woman that beautiful and genuine has to be taken, or if she isn't, she must have some sort of intimacy issues,* he thought. So the whole thing was gnawing at him. And now, to top things off, they were late. He wouldn't be able to hold the train much longer.

He reached for his cell phone, usually attached to his belt, but it wasn't there. He thought he must have left it in his suitcase and ran into his bedroom in the sleeping car to retrieve it. Sure enough, it was there. He saw several missed calls from Eve and started listening to his voice mail as he walked back out onto the platform.

Just as he was listening to her message, he saw Eve pushing Janet Thompson in a wheelchair. Roger was relieved and became impressed when he saw they had made the effort to dress in 1950s attire. He was struck by how much more beautiful Eve appeared than he remembered. At the sleeping car entrance, Eve started to help Janet out of the wheelchair while the redcap porter unloaded their luggage off the cart and onto the platform. Roger rushed over and helped Janet to her feet.

"Here, let me help."

"Thank you," Eve and Janet said simultaneously.

There was electricity as Roger and Eve made eye contact, smiled, and hugged each other. *Oh no,* she thought. *This feels even better than the last time.*

"I tried to call..."

"I know. I left my phone back in the room and just got your messages."

Porter Henry Wellington greeted Janet and Eve. "I'm your porter, Henry Wellington. It's my pleasure to serve you."

Henry started to load himself up with their luggage. Years of carrying heavy bags with handles had made his hands so arthritic that he had a hard time opening up his fingers enough to get a hold of the grips. However, once he got hold of the handles, he still exhibited great strength.

"Why, thank you, Henry. You're a dear," Janet said.

"Thank you, Henry," Eve said. She couldn't help but keep looking back at Roger. Roger lent his hand to help Janet and Eve up the sleeping car steps as the train conductor, wearing a navy blue uniform and hat, approached him.

"Ready, Mr. Storm?"

"Yes," Roger answered as he let go of Eve's hand, without looking at the conductor. Roger gave Eve a smile and then turned to the conductor and gave a confirming nod.

The conductor took out his train radio and strode away, saying into the device, "BNSF passenger extra to Harrison Street. We're ready to go west."

Suddenly, Roger remembered there was still one guest missing. He started to look again toward the entranceway, concerned.

A familiar voice called out to him from the other direction, toward the front of the train. "Roger!"

Roger turned around and saw Mr. Chapman, still wearing his porter's outfit, sitting on a suitcase in the middle of the platform. Roger ran up to him.

"Aren't you getting on?" Roger asked.

"No, Roger."

They were interrupted as the conductor yelled out at the end of the train, "All aboard!" The conductor then boarded the train and didn't see Roger still on the platform.

Roger stared at Mr. Chapman in disbelief. "You've gotten me to do all this, and now you're not even coming on the trip?"

"This is your journey, Roger."

At the front of the platform, a small signal went from horizontal to diagonal. The engineer notched out the throttle, and the three F-7 diesel units began pulsating into a louder melody. Imperceptibly, the nine stainless steel, streamlined cars began to move. The sight had the aura and sense of wonder likened to a majestic ocean liner on her maiden voyage.

Following the engines were the baggage-dormitory car, three sleeping cars, the dining car, the Pleasure Dome car, two more sleeping cars, and the rear Vista Canyon observation car. The engine horns blew loudly.

From the front of the platform, photographers and videographers took pictures, as the engines began to pass by.

Back on the platform, Roger glanced at the train picking up speed. He looked back to Mr. Chapman and hurriedly yelled, "But what's the purpose of all this?"

"I'm just the messenger, Roger. You'll find out in Lamy."

"What's in Lamy?"

"You'll see when you get there."

"What's with all the mystery? Just tell me what's in Lamy!" Roger demanded.

"I'm just taking orders. All in the Lord's timing. Now get on that train!"

Torn and irritated, Roger dashed a few feet and caught the last car. He looked back to see Mr. Chapman waving him on wistfully.

SANTA

Chapter Nine

THE JOURNEY BEGINS

How could Mr. Chapman not go on the ride? Let me just say he had his instructions. I hope you enjoy the journey…

Soon after leaving Union Station, the locomotive horn blew loudly in a salute to admirers on the Roosevelt Road Bridge. The train turned west onto the BNSF mainline and began to accelerate.

The train flew through the Illinois countryside in the late morning. Dozens of people stood by parked cars at various locations to admire it as it passed. Grandparents and parents shared stories with their children about the once-famous streamliner called "The Train of the Stars."

As the Super Chief moved through Princeton, Illinois, about one hundred rail fans stood outside the station to pay homage, cheer, and take photo after photo as the train rolled by. The passengers on board waved back to the onlookers.

Roger made a point of inviting Eve and Janet as his guests in the Super Chief dining car for an early dinner. The three of them sat together at a table that could seat four. The décor of Original Super Chief dining car 600, on loan from BNSF, was inspired by the rich hues of Native American art and the Southwestern landscape. Dozens of passengers oohed and aahed over the authentic interior design and table settings. Yellow rose buds, not yet opened, stood in the vases. A few modern-day celebrities sat at some of the other tables.

Wixie Wilson arrived at Roger, Eve, and Janet's table with glasses of wine. The train shook a little, and Wixie almost lost his balance. "I don't have the balance I used to," he declared with a smile. "In all the years, I'm proud to say I only lost my balance once." Wixie then started serving their drinks.

"When was that?" Roger asked.

"It was January 1, 1956. Grace Kelly walked by me in the dining car, and my knees buckled. She was royalty on wheels!"

Everyone laughed, and Wixie set a glass of wine before Janet.

"But then there was that other famous actress, Janet Thompson," Wixie added. Then he looked directly into Janet's eyes with a smile. "I wonder what ever happened to her?"

"I wondered if you'd remember, Wixie." Janet laughed and blushed.

"How could I ever forget the times you rode this train, and that fine movie you were in: *Save My Heart*?"

"Oh, dear! Not many people remember that film anymore," Janet confessed. Wixie perused the food-order slip they had filled out. Unlike in a normal restaurant, it was the custom in dining cars for the dinner guests to fill out their own order slips, which the waiters would leave on the table. The custom, started long before the advent of computer-generated meal checks, enabled an audit of kitchen and wait staff by green-eye-shaded bean counters back in the day. Wixie finished looking at the order slip Roger had filled out.

"Yes, sir! This ride is full of surprises. Everything looks good. I'll put your order in."

Wixie left and came back with their food a few minutes later. He carried a big tray and named each dish as he set each item before them. He served the food on the famous Mimbreno Indian-pattern Santa Fe China.

"Roast spring lamb with mint jelly," he said, placing the dish in front of Janet.

"Oh!" they all responded with delight.

"Grilled Lake Superior whitefish maître d'hôtel," he said of Eve's dish.

"Ooh."

"And filet mignon jardinière en casserole for Mr. Roger Storm."

"Ooh."

"Very nice presentation," Roger said.

They all took a moment to enjoy the display before them—the railroad version of *Babette's Feast.* The meal went rather long as they savored the cuisine and got reacquainted.

While they were eating, the Super Chief made a short stop in Kansas City, Missouri, and then proceeded on its way.

After they finished their main course, Wixie removed the plates from the table and put them on a tray. As Wixie was about to leave, he hesitated and looked quizzically at Roger. "Excuse me, Mr. Storm. You are the spittin' image of an engineer I knew."

Roger got uncomfortable and fidgeted in his chair. "Oh, really?" he responded.

"But his last name wasn't Storm," Wixie said. "It was Wickersham. George Wickersham."

"Yes. He was my father," Roger admitted, embarrassed.

"I knew it! I never forget a face." Wixie looked at another nearby waiter, Lee Gibson, and said, "I win the bet, Lee! This is George Wickersham's son."

"Yes, sir. George Wickersham, the engineer. He was a good man," Lee said.

"Yes, sir. He sure was," Wixie agreed. Then Wixie said to Roger, "He thought the world of you. He used to carry a picture of you and place it near the window when he was running up front."

"How do you know that?" Roger asked, incredulous.

"I took food up to the cab for him. Too bad about his eyesight. It was hard for him not to be an engineer anymore. But even to the end, he was thinking of others' well-being."

"What do you mean?" Roger asked.

"You know, how dedicated he was to his job and to those people."

Wixie noticed Lee motioning to him and knew he had to end the conversation. "Uh oh, the kitchen is calling," Wixie said, and he left.

Janet and Eve looked on curiously during the conversation, each for different reasons. Eve was fascinated to learn more information about Roger. She saw there was a hidden side to him. Janet was fascinated because she remembered something.

"He wore black-framed glasses?" Janet asked Roger.

"Yes," Roger said with a look of surprise, then confusion.

Janet looked thoughtful for a moment. Then she said to herself, "Wickersham."

Roger sat up straight when he heard her say that name.

"You changed your last name. Why?" she asked.

Roger looked down. "We weren't close. I didn't even know he kept my picture." He felt uncomfortable and was relieved when Violet Briggs approached, with Chester Young following, to interrupt their conversation.

"Mr. Storm! You won't believe what happened!" Violet noticed Janet and Eve there and said, "Oh, excuse me, ladies. Don't mind me; I'll just take a second." She turned back to Roger. "Chester here and I fell in love with each other on The Super Chief when we were teenagers. Can you believe that?"

Roger, Eve, and Janet smiled, caught up in her joy.

"That's amazing!" Roger said.

"But we never got together again," Violet added.

"She was my first love," Chester said.

"Isn't he just adorable!" Violet said.

"Even with my strange Vermont accent?"

Everyone laughed at Chester's remark.

"Why of course!" Violet exclaimed.

Janet's smile began to fade from the conversation as her eyes were drawn to a lone African American man in his thirties, sitting at a nearby table. The man sipped his coffee and stared at his cell phone. He wore an open-collared dress shirt and a nice sports coat. As she stared at him, her mind drifted back to her special trip.

It was 1944 in the Super Chief dining car, which was moving at night during wartime. Laughter filled the car as a similarly built, dashing, twenty-five-year-old African American man, Ernest, wearing a navy-blue Navy officer's ensign dress uniform, sat by himself at a table in the middle of the car.

The laughter came from other dinner guests, who were all white. Ernest, the only African American guest, noticed their disapproval.

At the end of the car, several white passengers waited in line. The dining car steward stood at the front of the line and was in charge of seating people. Two white couples were next in line. They had Texas accents and a Texas upbringing, which rejected the sight of a black man sitting in their perceived exclusive white domain, even with the uniform of the nation's military. Indeed, the officer's uniform added fuel to their perception of fire.

A single blonde woman, young Janet Thompson, twenty-three years old, was waiting behind them and saw Ernest seated by himself.

Young Janet, wearing a classic upscale 1940s dress, had a mischievous and confident personality, but below the surface, she was pure, innocent, and lonely.

The first couple complained loudly to the steward. "He should be back in the kitchen where he belongs," the husband said.

"I'm sorry, sir. The Santa Fe Railway does not run segregated trains. It will be a few minutes before other seats open up."

The steward looked at the second couple. "Two?"

"We're not sitting next to that Negro either," the second husband said.

Hearing all this, young Janet squinted disapprovingly and stepped forward. "Steward, I'll take a seat at that table," she said.

The two couples looked at her with a mixture of shock and disgust as she walked past them. The steward led her to the table where Ernest rose when she sat across from him. He was as surprised as anyone else.

She responded to his chivalry. "Your mother taught you well. Some men don't stand anymore when a woman comes to a table."

"My mother taught me a lot of things about…how to treat a beautiful lady, Ma'am."

"Did she teach you to be fresh?" she asked, amused.

"Only fresh as a daisy."

They both laughed, and she noticed the yellow roses in the table vase.

"Fresh as a daisy, not a rose?"

He laughed and said, "My daddy taught me well also. He said that when a man marries a woman, he must remember she is like a flower. If he is trustworthy and dependable, she will bloom. But if he is not, she will tend to wilt."

She looked at him and smiled, and then she caressed the lush, bright yellow roses.

Janet came back to the present, sixty years later, as she caressed similar yellow roses in a newer-looking vase. The train was moving in the late-afternoon sunlight. She looked over to the table where the African American man sat, but it was vacant now—just his coffee cup remained.

Janet hoped it wasn't too obvious to Eve and Roger that she had "spaced out." She'd noticed it happening to her more and more these past few years. She wondered where Violet and Chester had gone. She was relieved that Eve and Roger didn't appear concerned about her.

Wixie came and set desserts on their table. He noticed Janet caressing the roses while Roger and Eve looked preoccupied with messages on their cell phones. "They got all the details right on this trip, even down to the yellow roses," Wixie said. "The Super Chief always used fresh, closed yellow roses out of Chicago, which would fully bloom during the trip and stay fresh through to Los Angeles. Anything else you all need?"

Roger and Eve looked up from their cell phones. They hadn't been listening.

"Just give me the check," Roger said.

Wixie took out the check from his pocket. "I have it right here, young Mr. Wickersham."

"Storm," Roger corrected him.

"I mean Storm. Sorry," Wixie apologized.

"It's OK," Roger said.

Feeling self-conscious, Roger calculated the bill. He wondered what Eve and Janet thought of him.

Eve changed the subject. "I wanted to go up to the Pleasure Dome before it gets dark. Would you like to go, Mother?"

"No. I don't feel like climbing any stairs." Janet then winked to Eve. "You should get Roger to take you."

Roger looked up from the bill. "Oh, yes. I'd like to take you." He hoped he didn't appear too eager.

"I'm fine right here with my book," Janet said.

"Oh. OK," Eve said. She felt excited and guilty at the same time. *The dome car could be a romantic setting,* she thought.

Roger signed the check, but Eve noticed he'd signed it "Roger Wickersham" instead of "Roger Storm."

"Having an identity crisis?" she kidded, pointing to his mistake.

Roger, feeling embarrassed, said, "Ahh." Then he crossed out "Wickersham" on the check and replaced it with "Storm."

"You two, run along," Janet encouraged them. "I have *Pride and Prejudice* to keep me company."

"How many times have you read that book?" Eve teased her.

"Who's counting? Some things never get old."

Roger and Eve laughed and got up to leave.

The sun hung low in the sky as the Super Chief ran about ninety miles per hour through the Kansas countryside.

Roger and Eve found two empty rotating lounge chairs in the glass-enclosed dome of the Pleasure Dome car. The glass dome rose above the car's roof, giving guests a 360-degree view. They could see wheat fields in all directions, with wind making impressions in the fields. Several other couples occupied the remaining seats, including Violet and Chester, who sat together toward the front of the dome.

After Roger and Eve got comfortable, Roger wasn't quite sure where to start the conversation. He decided to keep the topic on Janet. "Were you able to find out anything more about that man she met on the train?"

"No. I'm still trying." After a moment, she asked, "So what's the story with you and your dad?" She immediately regretted asking the question. *Was that too personal? What am I doing?* she thought.

Roger was surprised she'd cut to the chase. *She is interesting. Most people wouldn't dare to ask that so soon,* he thought. Still, he felt uneasy with the subject. "Nothing much to tell. I heard he died years ago of a heart attack," he said.

"You heard?" She couldn't let it go.

"He hadn't been around in years. Only heard about it after my mother told me—long after the funeral."

Eve's eyes become moist. She wanted to know more. "And your mother?"

She isn't as closed off as I thought she might be, he thought. *Okay, I'll take the bait.*

"She died a few years ago—wealthy but unhappy. She'd turn over in her grave if she knew I spent all her money on this train."

Roger noticed Violet and Chester a few seats ahead, holding hands, and continued. "Look at them. They were on the list. Maybe this train is about answering peoples prayers and realizing their dreams. Maybe even dreams..."

"They didn't know they had," she finished.

Roger nodded.

"Mother's dream was to see that man again," Eve said. "What about you? Why do you think you're on here?" *I can't believe I keep asking him such personal questions. What's with me?* she thought.

"That's what disturbs me. I really don't know. All I know is, I'm supposed to find out in Lamy. You must think I'm crazy," he said.

"No. I'm intrigued."

He was surprised she'd said that. "What about you?" he asked.

"Remember, I wasn't on the list," she reminded him.

"Yes, but you were a package deal with your mother."

"I know I've always loved trains. Maybe that's why I'm here."

"And? There must be something more," he inquired.

I can't believe I'm going to say this, she thought. "OK. You can laugh now. When I was a little girl, I dreamed of someday meeting my husband on this train and having a candlelit dinner..."

"In the Turquoise Room," Roger finished the sentence for her.

She nodded and smiled. *How did he know?*

"Well, now you have your chance."

"No. Peter doesn't like trains." *Oh, what did you just do? Don't tell him about Peter yet. You're just getting to know him. Now you've blown it,* she thought.

Roger was a bit taken aback. "Peter?"

"We've been dating for five years." *I had to tell him,* she thought. *I was going to have to tell him sooner or later. I might as well have mentioned Peter now to get this over with, and we can go our separate ways.*

"But your mother said she was concerned because you don't have a man in your life."

"As far as she's concerned, I don't. She's never liked him."

Roger looked confused, trying to process this new information. *What is going on here?* he wondered. *I knew it was too good to be true that she was unattached.*

He and Eve saw Violet and Chester up ahead, playfully rubbing noses. As crazy as it seemed, as soon as they had begun their walk from the dining car to the Pleasure Dome car, Roger had begun hoping something romantic would happen between them in the dome. Now he was left looking at Violet and Chester rubbing noses. Roger wondered, *Why do things just work out so simply for some people?* He felt a cold bucket of water had just been poured on his head.

Eve felt bad. She was able to talk so easily to this man. Peter never opened up emotionally like this. *This man will never know now how much I wanted to hold his hand and look out together at the setting sun,* she thought. *But maybe it's for the best. Don't let your emotions run away with you. Remember, he's engaged!*

The train pulled up to the Dodge City, Kansas, station while it was still daylight. A few pleased onlookers applauded and took pictures. Then the train was again on its way.

* * *

While Eve and Roger were in the Pleasure Dome, Janet continued to sit at her table in the dining car, reading *Pride and Prejudice.* Wixie came to clear the table, and Janet looked up. She saw the dining car had become empty except for the steward and the kitchen crew eating at the far end.

"Did you ever see him again, Wixie?" she asked.

"Who's that?"

"You remember—Ernest."

"Oh, no, Miss Janet. I must say, that brother was born ahead of his time."

As Janet looked down at her half-eaten chocolate cake in front of her, her mind couldn't help but wander back to that evening in 1944.

After having dinner, Ernest and young Janet drank coffee with chocolate cake for dessert. A couple of glasses of water also sat on the table, near the small table vase with yellow roses.

The two couples from Texas sat at the table across the aisle from them, eavesdropping and glancing suspiciously at them throughout their conversation.

"When do you ship out?" young Janet asked.

"In three days."

"Are you scared?"

"I'd be crazy not to be. How about you?" he asked.

"It's scary going to an unknown place. My family thinks I'm crazy for wanting to be an actress in Hollywood. I've spent the whole trip second-guessing myself."

"I understand. My family thought I was crazy also, to report for duty by going on a train with rich white folk."

Young Janet looked at the two Texan couples and the other white folks around them, who were whispering about her and Ernest. She smiled at his casual manner.

"That's pretty brave of you," she said.

"It's also brave of you to go to Hollywood," Ernest said.

"Why does being brave have to be so lonely, Ernest?"

"If you really want to go after what you want, you have to be willing to let people think you're crazy." He was starting to feel his emotions well up inside him. "Look at most great people in history, Abraham Lincoln and Frederick Douglass believing in equality for all people. They were considered crazy by many of their peers. And to a lesser degree, it's the same way with our personal dreams. They can be met by a lot of opposition—even from those most close to us. Someday your family won't think you're crazy when you make it in the movies. And Lord willing, someday, a man like me riding on a white person's train won't appear crazy either."

"But the cost to you. I admire your bravery. You speak like a preacher."

Ernest laughed. "My daddy was a preacher..." Ernest's lightness faded, and he became more somber. "But the KKK got to him for talking to a white woman in public. She started visitin' his church, and that was the beginning of the end."

Her eyes moistened, confronted with the vulnerable reality of their own situation sitting together. "So your family would think you're crazy talking to me right now in public?"

"Most likely."

"I'll go, once I get my check."

"No. That's not what I meant. Please don't. I mean, I want to talk to you some more. Of course, as long as you do."

"I'd like that," she said.

"Then let's move somewhere else," he suggested.

"That would be nice."

Young Janet touched the yellow roses again in the table vase and smiled. Ernest noticed her pleasure in the flowers.

At the same time, the couples from Texas were beginning to feel the effects of their cocktails and began looking at Ernest and young Janet more intensely.

The waiter, twenty-three-year-old Wixie Wilson, brought their checks. Ernest and Young Janet started to put money down.

Young Wixie looked at Ernest and spoke softly. "I must say, besides Louis Armstrong and Fats Waller, you're the only colored man I've served on this train."

"And now Fats is dead, so there's just me and Louis."

"You know, poor Fats died right here on the Super Chief last December from a heart attack," young Wixie said.

"Yes, I heard," Ernest nodded.

"And even he wasn't treated all too kindly on here. Watch your back," young Wixie said.

Ernest and young Janet looked thoughtfully at each other. Young Wixie started to leave before being interrupted by the bigoted Texas husband, who spoke loudly and tried to make eye contact with Ernest.

"Hey, waiter. It sure does stink in here. Is there anything you can do about it?"

The wives laughed.

"That stink needs to go to a Jim Crow car," the other husband said.

Ernest and Janet looked away. From a distance, the concerned steward looked on.

"Ain't none of those on this train. It should go away soon, sir," young Wixie said. Then Wixie turned, looked at Ernest with concern, and exited.

"I think I better go first," Ernest whispered to young Janet. "We shouldn't leave together."

Turning his back to the couples, Ernest slyly took the yellow roses from the vase, put them into his pocket, and got up to leave. The bigoted husband caught his eye.

"Boy, you sure are lucky this train doesn't go through Texas, or you'd be thrown off."

They laughed. Ernest restrained his anger and did not engage them as he walked away. Young Janet looked down at her dessert plate, half a piece of uneaten chocolate cake still on it.

Young Wixie came back carrying a water pitcher. "Are you finished, ma'am?" he asked young Janet.

"Yes. Just some more water."

Young Wixie started to pour water into her glass. After he filled it, she said, "Both glasses, please."

Young Wixie paused and raised his eyebrows at Young Janet.

"Pour it, Wixie."

"Yes, ma'am."

Young Wixie poured water into the second glass.

"Oh, waiter," the first Texas wife said, "there's a blonde stink on here also."

"I think it's cheap trash," the other wife added.

They laughed. Young Wixie ignored their comments and left.

After a few moments, young Janet got up from the table calmly and turned her back to the couples. Then she took the two full glasses of water from her table, turned around, and threw the water into their faces. She put the glasses back down and started to leave. The couples were aghast, too shocked to respond immediately.

Eve's voice brought Janet back to the present. "Are you ready to leave?" she asked after returning from the Pleasure Dome car without Roger. Eve stood by the table, and the dining car was now empty except for the steward doing paperwork at a table at the end.

Janet saw it was dark outside now as the train moved through the night. She finished drinking a glass of water with a smirk on her face, still thinking of her daring act as a young woman.

"Oh, I'm sorry! Yes, dear."

Eve helped her up. "It's past nine. We need to get you to bed."

* * *

Later that evening, as the lighted train swept across the darkened Kansas plains, Roger was in his bedroom, tossing in his sleep. He was having a hard time dealing with his earlier conversation with Eve. He'd left things with her polite and cordial, but he still felt frustrated. He kept trying to relax.

He could hear the engine's horn blow outside, which brought him back to another distant memory.

It was 1968, and young Roger was seven years old. He sat eating dinner at the kitchen table with his mother at his dad's home in the hills of Glorieta, New Mexico, before the family broke up. Young Roger heard the train engine horn blow.

"There's your father," Marlene said, disinterested.

Young Roger got up quickly and grabbed a high-powered flashlight next to the door and ran outside the front of the house to a dirt road. He turned left and dashed up the road about one hundred yards to a trailhead on the left side. He bolted up the path and didn't stop until he came to a rustic bench, which overlooked a canyon pass.

As the Super Chief wound through the pass below, young Roger stood on the bench and waved the flashlight toward the train.

From the moving train, George opened the side engine door and waved his lantern in return. Young Roger continued waving the flashlight up on the hill, jumping up and down excitedly on the bench.

Roger, still in his sleep, shook his arms like young Roger, waking himself from his memory that had turned into a dream. He sat up, startled. If it wasn't thoughts about Eve, then it was now thoughts about his dad that kept him up. He wondered if he would ever get any sleep that night.

He didn't, so he got up early and went to the Pleasure Dome to watch the sun rise over the hilly Colorado countryside.

When it was time for breakfast, Roger went to the dining car and sat by himself. Chester Young and Violet Briggs later joined him when they found him sitting alone. They all ordered the famous French toast with the crust cut off, shaped in triangles. It was very puffy with a custard-like center and covered with confectioner's sugar. Chester had brought along his own jug of Vermont maple syrup. When Chester and Violet started eating it, they moaned as if they might be having orgasms, making eyes at each other. Roger ate it also, but with less excitement than the two "teenagers in love."

"Can you believe this?" Chester blurted out.

"It tastes exactly the same—especially with your homemade Vermont maple syrup," Violet said. Turning to Roger, she said, "That's one of the cute things I remember about Chester when we were young: he said he brought his own supply of maple syrup wherever he went."

"Only Vermont Fancy Grade will do—never leave home without it," Chester said.

"You're a true Vermonter," Roger said.

"Yes. Don't see much point in leaving there often. You'll never find a prettier state."

Chester looked out at the vast landscape near La Junta, Colorado. "Though I must say, there's a lot more space out here," he said. "Reminds me of the time the Vermont farmer visited the Colorado rancher on his property. The rancher was real proud of his acreage and wanted to impress the Vermont farmer, so he said, 'Why it takes me a whole day to drive from one end of my property to the other.' The Vermonter, unimpressed, said, 'Yup. I once had a truck like that...but I got rid of it.'"

Roger and Violet laughed.

"I told you, he is so cute," Violet said, as she pinched his cheek. "A regular comedian."

Chester blushed.

"Why didn't you two get married?" Roger asked.

"Daddy wouldn't permit it," Violet said.

"Took a long time to get over you," Chester said, getting a little teary-eyed.

Violet was about to cry also.

Roger tried to lighten the mood. "Well, I'm happy you two found each other again!"

As Roger looked up, he saw a distinguished elderly Caucasian gentleman rise from another table. With white hair and a trimmed white beard, the gentleman wore a three-piece suit with a red rose on his lapel. He proceeded to leave the car.

The rose, Roger thought. He excused himself from Violet and Chester and hurried to catch up to the gentleman. Roger approached him in the sleeping car corridor.

"Excuse me, sir. This is gonna seem like an odd question, but, years ago, did you ever happen to meet a young actress on the Super Chief by the name of Janet Thompson?"

"Was she pretty?"

"Yes."

"Hmm..." the gentleman hesitated. "No, but I wish I had. Sounds like it could have been exciting!" The man walked on.

Roger shook his head. He thought he had found Janet's old flame wearing a rose.

* * *

An hour later, the train was approaching Trinidad, Colorado. Eve and Janet were returning from a late breakfast in the dining car. Eve held Janet's hand, helping her through the car door into the sleeping car's vestibule. Janet held a cane in her other hand to help support herself. She paused for a moment to catch her breath, and then looked around with a smile. She remembered how the Dutch-style doors could open.

"Wait, honey," she said. "Could you open the top half of that door? I'd like to get some fresh air."

Eve nodded and pulled open the top half of the vestibule door.

As the wind blew through Janet's hair, she remembered someone else who had opened up a vestibule door for her in 1944.

It was Ernest, a few minutes after she had thrown the water on the two nasty couples. They were smoking in the vestibule, laughing and enjoying each other's company. She held the yellow roses he had given her.

A white male passenger walked through the door between cars, and they suddenly became quiet. The passenger glared at them momentarily and then continued on to the next car. The door closed behind him, and they laughed again. Then they became quiet and listened to the clickety-clack of the train wheels.

Ernest seemed to be pondering something and took a deep breath. "Are you a night owl?" he asked.

"It depends on the night."

"Tomorrow night," Ernest suggested. "Meet me at midnight in the rear observation car. By then, everyone's gone and we can talk."

"I'd like that."

In unison, they seemed to know it was time to go. They walked into the sleeping car corridor. She led the way and he followed. Young Janet got to her room first and stopped. Ernest waited behind her.

"This is me."

"I'm just a few doors down," he said, pointing.

"How convenient," she mused. "Good night."

"Good night."

They smiled but didn't touch each other. Ernest walked on to his room.

Before entering her room, young Janet looked back at him. She noticed his disposition change as he looked wearily at his door.

Curious, she came up behind him to see what he was looking at. Someone had harshly streaked "Nigger Room" on the door with black shoe polish. Her face turned to a mixture of fear and sadness.

"I'm sorry."

"Guess I should have expected it," Ernest said.

A porter approached with cleaning supplies. "I just saw it," he said. "I'm taking care of it, sir. Your room is made up."

"Thank you," Ernest responded.

Ernest looked back and nodded at young Janet. She looked concerned and then turned back to go into her room. Ernest entered his room and closed the door behind him, and the porter started washing off the writing.

Back in the present, Janet and Eve made their way from the vestibule to the sleeping car corridor.

"Mother, I forgot the name of that man you met on the Super Chief," Eve said.

Janet seemed preoccupied and didn't answer right away. As Eve opened their bedroom door, Janet gazed wistfully at the clean door with new paint. Her eyes became moist. "His name was Ernest."

Eve opened the door wider to let her mother pass. Then she closed the door behind them, not knowing the significance to Janet of a cleanly painted bedroom door.

Climbing to the New Mexico state line, the Super Chief made the ascent to Raton Pass. After going through a half-mile tunnel, the train came out into the sunlight where a sign read, "Raton Tunnel—Highest Point On The Santa Fe: 7,588' Elevation." A mixture of green pine trees and pink-colored rocks dominated the New Mexico landscape.

* * *

A couple of hours later, the train passed Las Vegas, New Mexico, and then continued west, where a distinctive flat-topped, rock-capped mesa, Starvation Peak, came into view.

Roger and Dena sat drinking coffee at the rear of the elegant round-end observation car. She wore a pretty Native American/South Western-style dress that fit in nicely with the decorated interior of Navajo art on the walls and embroidery on the stuffed chairs. At the bar, located at the front end of the car, a bartender made drinks. Guests filled the lounge area in the middle portion of the car.

Roger and Dena looked out the window at Starvation Peak.

"My father used to tell me the legend about Starvation Peak," Dena said.

"That flat-topped rock?"

"Yes," she continued. "In the early 1800s, it became the last stand for thirty Spanish settlers after they tried to steal Navajo land. My people chased them off their land and up the mountain before the settlers fought the Navajo off by throwing rocks down at them. Instead of trying to get to the top and fight, my people surrounded the peak and let the settlers starve to death."

"On that note, I think I'm ready for lunch," Roger joked.

She laughed and then looked out the side window as the train rounded a curve. "Look at that," she said. "You can see the whole train."

The Super Chief wound sharply downhill through a huge double S-curve, allowing the passengers to see both ends of the train.

After they looked out, Roger noticed she seemed nervous and preoccupied.

"Are you doing OK?"

Dena nodded. "Coming up to Lamy though…"

"What happened in Lamy?"

"It wasn't pleasant," she said. Then she paused, obviously troubled by something. "Maybe some other time…"

"Sure, some other time then." Roger didn't want to push it.

At the lounge front entrance, Eve entered, looking for Roger. He rose as he saw her.

"She's here. I'll catch you later," he said to Dena, and she nodded.

Eve and Dena exchanged smiles as Roger escorted Eve away.

Roger and Eve went back to the Pleasure Dome car and climbed upstairs to sit in the dome. Eve took pictures of the beautiful New Mexico scenery. The train weaved through a spectacular granite gorge, Apache Canyon, so narrow the rock at times was just a couple of feet from the train, and high cliffs of red rocks hovered over the Super Chief.

The conductor came upstairs to the dome to make an announcement. "Our next stop will be Lamy, New Mexico, in ten minutes. Lamy is the stop for nearby Santa Fe. We'll be making a special one-night stopover in Lamy, so those who want to can take a connecting tourist train into Santa Fe to do some sightseeing."

After the conductor went downstairs, Eve updated Roger on Janet. "She said she doesn't want to go into Santa Fe, but she wants me to go with you. What is it with you? You must have really charmed her."

"I didn't charm you?"

She smiled and then looked away. "That's…not relevant."

"Did you find out anything more about her gentleman friend?" Roger asked.

"Are you always this determined?"

"Only when I have to be."

"His name was Ernest, and he was shipped off to the Pacific Fleet during World War II. They were to each wear yellow roses."

"Yellow!" Roger exclaimed. "Ernest?" Roger pulled the two-page guest list from his suit-coat pocket and quickly scanned it. He looked perturbed. "No. No Ernest. What's up with all this?"

"Maybe we'll find out…"

"In Lamy," they said in unison as the train approached the Lamy station.

LAMY

Chapter Ten

A STOP IN LAMY AND SANTA FE

What was going to happen in Lamy? All in due time, my friend…

The small station sat by itself in the midst of the rolling desert hills dotted with small pinyon trees. Besides having an inside lobby, one side of the station featured an outdoor covered-porch waiting area.

Nearby, an unused siding held an old railroad dining car, which operated as a restaurant. About fifty automobiles sat parked in the adjacent dirt parking lot. A waiting spur line train to Santa Fe sat further up the siding. It had one engine that read, "Santa Fe Southern Railroad" with three coaches attached. The only other building in town, The Legal Tender Saloon & Restaurant, was located across the dirt road and provided the social center for the 200 plus residents in town.

A small, old-fashioned band, complete with red-and-white-striped suits, played some Souza marches for the occasion. About one hundred spectators clapped at the train's arrival.

Roger and Eve disembarked together and stretched their legs. Roger, not knowing what to look for, strolled further down the platform with Eve following close behind. Seeing nothing, Roger and Eve joined the other passengers, who were walking toward the waiting spur line train.

When Dena stepped off the Super Chief a half-hour later, the crowd had dispersed. The locals had gone home in their cars, and most of the other passengers had boarded the spur line train and were waiting for it to leave. Dena walked steadily toward the station and sat on a bench near the building. She looked at a small metal plaque on the outside wall.

At that moment, the spur line train headed out, pulling the three coaches. Soon the station area became very quiet.

Dena stayed seated on the bench. Unseen by her, a large Native American man, Dasan, walked up close behind her and stared at her. He had long black-and-gray hair, held with a wide band around his forehead. He waited for his daughter to turn around.

He thought about what he would say to her. It had been five years since she'd left the reservation, and they had exchanged heated words. She had been frustrated with his drinking ever since her mother had died. Dasan had been in denial about how alcohol was destroying their family. He had never gotten violent, but he would end up passed out somewhere, and Dena would have to go get him and put him to bed.

By continuing to live in that environment, Dena feared she might end up addicted to alcohol, like many of her friends and family, so she felt she had to get away.

Dasan wanted to tell her he had been sober for three years now. It seemed like an eternity before she turned around, but when she did, he gathered up the courage to come clean with his daughter.

* * *

Back on the spur line train to Santa Fe, Roger and Eve sat together on a car filled with passengers. The Lamy station was only twenty miles from downtown Santa Fe, but it still took the spur line train about an hour to get there because of reduced speed limits over the old desert track.

After they disembarked at the Santa Fe Depot, they browsed through a bookstore at the nearby Sambusco Market to find a new large-print book for Janet. Roger then gave Eve a walking tour of the town by heading up Guadalupe Street and then over toward Canyon Road. They kept the conversation light as they just enjoyed being in each other's company. *Some things just come naturally*, Roger thought. Eve also noticed how easy it was to communicate with him.

When they walked along Canyon Road, they had the opportunity to visit numerous art galleries and cute shops. Having such a simple outing allowed them to learn new things about each other such as their love for beauty and art. She tended to like modern styles while he liked traditional landscape paintings. They playfully bantered back and forth about the superiority of their individual taste over the other. Eve appreciated a man who had a variety of interests. Her fiancé Peter was all business.

Eventually they made their way back toward downtown along the Western-style San Francisco Avenue. Having walked several miles, they stopped for a meal at the La Plazuela Restaurant in the adobe-style La Fonda Hotel. She liked the fact that Roger only had one drink during dinner. She had become tired of always telling Peter to stop after four or five.

The sun was setting as they strolled after dinner across the quaint Santa Fe Plaza—a park surrounded by old Western-style adobe storefronts. Roger felt an urge to find out more about Peter.

"Why doesn't your mother like Peter?"

He cut to the chase. Interesting, she thought. "She's afraid he's too much like my father, who had a wandering eye. We both had to forgive my father for a lot of things. What's sad for me is that she just wanted a man to really love her and adore her. I think that's what most women want."

"Is that what you want?"

Eve nodded. "Peter and I had some problems a few months ago."

"Another woman?"

She nodded again. *He is smart,* she thought.

"Its one of the worst feelings—being cheated on."

"Tell me about it, Doctor Roger," she teased him. "You seem to speak from experience."

Roger smiled and nodded. "It makes you wonder deep down if you can ever really…"

"Trust them again."

"Exactly," Roger said.

"I forgave him, but still…"

"It changes things."

"Exactly," she said. She had a quizzical look of enchantment on her face. "I'm not used to someone being able to finish my thoughts." She knew what he was about to say, so they said it together:

"Me, either!"

They laughed awkwardly, knowing this was a mystical moment.

"Do you do this with all the women?" she asked.

"Only the slow ones."

She playfully slapped him on the shoulder.

What are you doing? she thought. *Don't forget—he's engaged to be married. I wonder why he hasn't mentioned her?*

"When are you supposed to get married?" she asked.

"We were, in the fall."

"Were?" Eve tried not to sound too excited.

"The engagement's off."

"Why?"

"Different values. She called it off, but then I realized I wasn't in love with her. I met someone else."

"You did?" Now she was really confused.

"But she's taken."

"Your assistant?" she concluded.

"Who?" he asked, perplexed for a moment. "No. Dena's like a little sister to me."

"Oh. She's pretty."

Roger looked into her eyes and decided to let the cat out of the bag. "You *are* slow."

She was flustered and excited at the same time. "Oh…maybe she's not as taken as you think, if you just pursued her."

"Do you think that's what I need to do?"

"Maybe you can capture her heart." *I can't believe I just said that. It's so corny!* she thought.

They looked into each other's eyes, the questions playing.

"Do you think she would join me in the Turquoise Room tomorrow for dinner?"

Excited despite herself, she blushed. "It would have to be after her mother goes to bed."

"Around ten p.m.?"

She nodded and smiled.

They got back to the Santa Fe Station that night at ten, just in time to take the return trip on the spur line back to Lamy. Since the Super Chief wasn't scheduled to leave Lamy until noon the next day, they could have opted to stay overnight like some other passengers at a hotel in Santa Fe; however, Eve didn't want to leave her mother by herself, so they went back in the evening.

Once off the spur line coach in Lamy, Roger escorted Eve on the short walk over to her sleeping car on the Super Chief. He thought, *I wonder if I should hold her hand? No, don't rush things. It will be nice to hug her again soon, though.*

On her part, Eve enjoyed walking near him and the smell of his cologne. She wondered, *Will he try to hold my hand? I guess not. I like that. He's not trying to rush things.*

Roger gave her a hug goodnight at the stairwell of her car. This hug lasted longer than the others, but he didn't try to kiss her.

When Eve got back to her room, Janet lay awake reading in bed. "How was Santa Fe?"

"It was fine."

"Did you have a nice time with him?"

"Yes, Mother. He was very nice. You were right."

Janet chuckled. She enjoyed seeing her daughter exhibit a vibrant glow on her face. After Eve changed into her pajamas and climbed up the stepladder to her berth, Janet turned off her reading light. Both of them rested in silence.

"I was praying for the two of you," Janet said in the dark.

"What?" Eve said. She bent over the side of the bed and looked down at her mother. "I've never heard you say you 'pray.' What's gotten into you?"

"Desperate times require desperate measures."

They both giggled.

"You are too much! My mother—Maria von Trapp!"

They laughed some more and rested peacefully that night.

* * *

After leaving Eve, Roger took a walk along the dimly lit brick station platform that stretched much further East than necessary because it once provided access to the upscale El Ortiz Hotel, destroyed many years before. A gentle breeze swept through the trees that grew over the old foundation, causing a sound that Roger likened to a person moaning. Standing in pure darkness, the station and parked train in the distance seemed much brighter to Roger than before. Thoughts about his day with Eve brought a smile to his face. *Maybe something can happen with us. What a nice surprise that would be, he thought. I can't believe how relaxed and at home I feel with her.*

He was also surprised at how comfortable and at home he felt being in Lamy and Santa Fe. Sure, he had grown up there, but he never previously had a desire to return. As he strolled back toward the train, he sat on a bench, near the station entrance. The station wall and small plaque were in shadows. Even though things went great with Eve, he still wondered what the trip was about.

After resting a few moments, Roger noticed through the station windows that the lights were still on in The Legal Tender Saloon & Restaurant across the street. He thought maybe he could find a clue there that might provide more clarity, so he decided he would go over and investigate.

He vaguely remembered the place as a child when his parents would take him to dinner there on special occasions. When Roger stepped inside, however, he had forgotten how elegant the 1881 structure was—complete with a long cherry wood bar imported from Germany and a Victorian-style dining room. A few customers sat at tables while a young guitarist provided music.

Roger sat at the empty bar. He found the music soothing. The middle-aged bearded bartender served Roger a draft beer.

"You part of the train group?

Roger nodded.

"I think I scared some of your group off earlier this evening," he said with a chuckle as he dried some glasses with a towel.

"How is that?

"Oh, I just told them some of the rumors about this place over the decades. Some people swear they've seen ghosts. I've been here for twenty years, and I've never seen anything. There's supposed to be a lady in a white gown floating around and a little girl sitting by herself on the stairs. Someone said they saw a man in black helping himself to a drink—truth be known, that may have been me when I was closing up one night after a long day and I treated myself." The bartender laughed. "Catch my drift?"

Roger nodded.

"No, I don't buy all the ghost stuff…now angels are another matter. I do believe in angels."

"Why is that?"

"Angels have a purpose. They are supposed to be protectors and messengers for us. The whole idea of ghosts never attracted me—that's not to say they don't exist. They just seem to be caught up in their own narcissistic issues and can't let go. I'm not sure what good that does anybody. 'C'mon, get over it,' is what I'd say to them. 'Move on to what's next. Leave your past behind.'"

Roger smiled and nodded. "Life is a mystery at times."

"Where are you from?" the bartender asked.

"I grew up nearby in Glorietta. Haven't been here in years."

"Well, you didn't miss much. I could probably give you all the news on the front page of a paper."

Roger snickered and then took a moment to collect his thoughts and to figure out how to phrase the question on his mind. "Now that you mention it, I was just wondering…

has anything noteworthy happened here? Is Lamy known for something special?"

The bartender looked at him blankly. "No, Amtrak stops here twice a day. That's about it. People drive from Santa Fe to eat here and go to the railroad museum. Not much out here anymore. I hear in the old days, when the town was larger, there was the occasional robbery. There's been talk recently of New Mexico not wanting to pay to maintain the track on this line. I'd hate to see the railroad go." He finished drying the glasses and gave Roger a wink. "You might ask one of the ghosts—maybe they would know if something special ever happened here."

Roger nodded, and the bartender left to return to the kitchen. Roger sat by himself for a few more minutes until the guitarist finished playing and the other patrons exited. He gave one more look around the place and concluded there was nothing to learn there about the purpose of his trip. On his walk back to the Super Chief though, he decided there might be one more place he could find the answer.

* * *

Early the next morning, Roger arranged for the one taxi service covering Lamy to pick him up at the station and drive him to the house where he grew up in the town of Glorieta, about sixteen miles away. He didn't know why, but he thought maybe the answer was out there, since that was the place he knew best as a kid.

He decided to wait until later to take a shower in the specially designed shower added to the sleeping car—one of the few modernizations from the original train— and then change into a suit before the train departed. That being the case, he looked a bit tired and unkempt when the old taxi arrived. Wearing jeans and a t-shirt, he sported a day's growth and forgot to comb his hair. The high-mileage taxi wasn't in much better condition, with missing hubcaps and an exterior that appeared as if it hadn't been washed in months.

Roger hadn't seen the house since the last time he visited his dad when he was nine years old. He didn't know how hard it would be to find it.

"You don't have an address?" the weary forty-year-old Hispanic driver said.

"I'll know it when I see it. Just drive towards Glorieta."

The driver hesitated and assessed Roger in the rear-view mirror—making sure Roger looked trustworthy—and shook his head. "It's your dime. You remember: I only take cash."

"Yes, you don't have to worry," Roger assured him.

The car still did not move. "I have to be careful, you know—I've been burned a number of times, picking up passengers, even rich Anglos, who want me to drive to a remote location and then they don't have enough cash. They tell me, they'll send it in the mail, but they never do. Ain't worth the gas to go track them down."

"I can imagine." Roger took the hint and removed a hundred dollar bill from his wallet and handed it to him. "This should cover it."

The driver nodded, relaxed, and smiled. "Ah, I figured you were good for it, my friend." The driver started out and was more motivated for the rest of the trip.

Roger remembered the house technically was in the Santa Fe National Forest, but it had a Glorieta postal address. After the taxi reached I-25 and drove East for a few miles, Roger had the driver take an exit outside Glorieta. They came across a dirt road called Deva Lane.

"Yes, that's it," Roger said.

The driver nodded and made an abrupt right turn. The car spewed up dust along the road and the driver slowed occasionally for an unfavorable rock or gulley. Roger straightened up in the back seat, surveying the area. When they came to the end of the road, Roger still hadn't found the house. He knew it had to be there. The taxi circled back again, but still no house. He asked the driver to stop at what seemed like a familiar setting, though more overgrown, and wait for him while he walked around. He noticed a bare area that looked like it could have once been a driveway. Surely, the house should be here, Roger thought. He investigated further inland and noticed the remains of a charred foundation, obviously scorched by fire, camouflaged by a mixture of weeds and mounds of windswept red sand. He walked around the foundation and remembered where each room would have been. It wasn't until he stood in front of what was once the fireplace, that he had an emotional reaction. It brought him to a dark place. A gust of wind suddenly blew a tumble weed into him, scratching his arm. He reflected how it was a symbolic reminder that his life really didn't seem to matter—there was little evidence to suggest that he even once lived there. It was as if his childhood never existed. A tear came to his eye.

Roger soon returned to the taxi where he found the driver leaning his head back against the headrest with the engine off.

Through the open window, the driver told him, "I remember now—that place burned down years ago. I think it was arson."

Roger opened the door and was about to enter, when he remembered something. He looked down the road toward the path.

"Can you wait here a little longer?"

"Sure, it's your dime."

Roger walked briskly down the road to the trail entrance and scurried up the path. He approached the place where the bench once stood—the bench he didn't reach when his mother chased him down on the day they moved.

At first, he saw no evidence of the bench until he noticed a section of it resting under a nearby shrub, hardly recognizable. Roger lifted it and saw pieces were still attached with rusty nails.

He remembered as if it were yesterday when his dad let him help build the rustic-style wooden bench at age seven in the garage. His dad held a piece in place while Roger tried to pound in a nail.

"That's it. Just give it a few more whacks." Roger finished, and George turned it over.

"Where are we going to put this, Daddy?"

"You'll see. Follow me." George picked up the bench and walked outside. Roger followed him down the road and out to the end of the path. "We're going to put it here."

"Why here?"

"It's for you to sit on when you want to find me passing in the train below. I'll see you when you wave during the day or when you use a flashlight at night. You can come to the bench to find me. And you'll be able to see me waving from the side door of the engine."

Back to the present, Roger held the broken piece and gazed out at the view overlooking the winding railroad track cutting through the valley below—the same track where he rode on the Super Chief as it entered Lamy the day before. Bitter feelings rose inside him, and he wildly threw the broken piece of the bench as far away as he could. He threw it so hard that his upper arm hurt, and he grabbed his sore arm with his other hand to sooth the throbbing. He calmed down after a few minutes as he continued to stand at the same spot. He still didn't know what the purpose of the trip was, and he could see the answer was not going to be forthcoming near his old homestead. *What did I think I'd learn by coming here? The purpose of the trip has nothing to do with this place. I should have known. Mr. Chapman said I would find out the purpose of this trip in Lamy, not Glorieta.*

He returned to the taxi and arrived back in Lamy an hour before departure.

* * *

Roger's patience wore thin concerning Mr. Chapman's directions. It didn't seem likely he would find out the purpose of the trip in Lamy either. To relieve his nerves, he took a final stroll around the Lamy station before the parked Super Chief was due to depart at noon. Many of the other passengers also stretched their legs before having to board for the rest of the trip.

The conductor called out, "Thirty minutes!"

Near the outside station entrance, Dena and her father, Dasan, stood together holding flowers and facing a commemorative wall plaque—the same plaque Dena had looked at from the bench the day before.

Further down the platform, Roger continued strolling, observing the station and surrounding scenery. His cell phone vibrated in his belt case holder. He took it out and looked at the screen: "Unavailable Funds Alert in Checking Account ******8843." He appeared stressed, took a deep breath, and exhaled before putting the cell phone back in its case.

Then, something caught his eye: Dena and Dasan were placing flowers under that plaque on the outside wall of the station. Roger kept his distance, but he was curious. Dena had briefly introduced Roger to her father earlier that morning, but they hadn't gotten a chance to share much. Roger had excused himself because he didn't want to intrude upon their time together.

Dasan stared at Roger and whispered in Dena's ear. Dena motioned Roger over, and he walked up to them.

Meanwhile, at a bench in the background, Eve and Janet sat reading—Janet from her new book, and Eve from her iPad. Eve looked up and noticed Roger talking to Dena and Dasan, but she couldn't hear what they were saying.

"Dasan," Roger began, "I still can't get over how you knew Dena would be here."

"A father can feel the spirit of his child," Dasan said.

Dena changed the topic. "Roger, you asked me before what happened here. My father says he wants to tell you."

"If that's all right, but don't feel you have to," Roger said.

"Roger," Dasan began slowly, "Dena's mother and I took Dena on a trip here when she was a small child. Lamy was known to be a bit wild back then. We were waiting for a train to go back to the res. inside the station on a cold night. We were the only passengers in the lobby. Suddenly two drunken men came into the station with guns; they held up the ticket agent. After getting the money, they shot him. Then they shot me in the thigh. I couldn't move."

Roger looked shocked. Tears came to Dasan and Dena's eyes.

"Then they tried to rape my wife, who was holding onto Dena. They pointed the gun right at her—for her to let Dena go."

"I'm sorry. I had no idea," Roger said.

"The injured ticket agent came out and jumped the men from behind. He put up a fight, but they shot him again and killed him. Just then, we heard a police car siren and they ran out. If it hadn't been for that ticket agent disrupting them, we might not have survived."

"I can see why you wouldn't want to relive it."

"But it's important to remember what that man did," Dena said.

Dasan stared oddly at Roger. "His spirit is here. I feel it," Dasan said.

"Who?" Roger asked.

Dasan pointed to the plaque on the wall.

Roger curiously walked up to it and read, "'In Memory of George Wickersham, for his faithful service to the Santa Fe Railway and to Amtrak.' My father."

Tears came to Roger's eyes. He was beside himself and started to breathe heavily. He then began to pace, gasping for air. He felt his whole world had been tossed upside down. A few moments later, he collapsed on the bench. Dasan and Dena tried to comfort him and put their hands on his shoulders.

Eve had observed all this and came over to see what was wrong, leaving Janet to watch the commotion from the far bench.

When Dena saw Eve approaching, she motioned her over to speak to her on the side. After Dena explained what had happened, she left with her father. Eve then sat next to Roger, who looked dazed, not knowing what to say to him.

After a moment, she said, "Dena told me. I'm sorry."

Roger nodded and just sat there, silently looking at the plaque. After a few moments, he finally said, "I never knew... last I heard was that he was an engineer. I didn't even know that he became a ticket agent. What do I do when I've held so much anger against him, and then I find this out?"

He bolted up and started pacing again, directing his frustration toward the plaque. Eve looked on with sympathy.

"Now I find out he died like some kind of hero. Great! But he never lifted a finger to see me... This is what this trip is all about? I'm just supposed to feel guilty now?"

"There must be something more to this," Eve said.

"Yeah. Seven million dollars more! I knew all this was too good to be true. Brook was right. I was crazy to do this. Nothing is in this for me."

Eve looked at him dejectedly. "Nothing?"

"Nothing."

"What about…us meeting?" Eve asked.

"Us? Let's quit dreaming! This is all nothing! People say life's about showing up. It's not. It's about people leaving. People are always going to leave you—it's just a matter of when. Look, I have to come clean with you: I'm broke. This trip has wiped me out. I've found women ultimately are only attracted to a guy if he has money, so let's just stop it right here. I have nothing to give you! So you're going to go back to Peter, and I'm going back to…I don't know what. Nothing! Just leave me alone."

Tears streamed down Eve's face, and she sadly walked away.

Roger continued, hunched over by himself for a few minutes until Janet walked up behind him.

"Roger, you were the boy who threw the model train engine on the lobby floor at Union Station."

Roger turned around, looking incredulous. "What? You were there?"

"I talked to your father after your mother took you away."

Janet became unsteady as her hands shook, holding the cane. Roger jumped up to take her hand.

"Here, let me." He led her to sit down. "Are you all right?"

"Just feeling a little light-headed," she said, and smiled at Roger. "I'm fine."

"How could you remember a short conversation from forty years ago?"

"He made an impression on me, dressed in his engineer's outfit," she continued. "It was nice to see a father who loved his son."

"Doesn't sound like the father I knew."

"I invited him to lunch with Eve and me while we waited for the next train. I thought he could use some encouragement."

"Are you sure? This just seems too bizarre to be true."

"Eve was just a little girl. She barely remembers it, but she picked up the pieces of your train engine and gave them back to your dad."

Roger shook his head in guilt and exasperation. "I thought he was being mean to my mother—at least that's what she said."

Their conversation was interrupted as they heard the conductor yell, "All aboard!" from the train platform.

After the announcement, Roger escorted Janet back to the sleeping car. On the way, he said, "I'm sorry; I hurt your daughter. I need to apologize to her."

"That would be nice. Just give her a little time."

Up ahead at the engine, a train engineer dressed in coveralls climbed up to the cab with polished experience.

Chapter Eleven

THE JOURNEY RESUMES

You can't believe Janet could remember that incident from forty years ago...I guess that makes you like Roger. But let me tell you, she had a sharp mind. Aren't there some things you can remember vividly from forty years ago? I know I can.

As far as you not believing Roger hadn't previously done any research on his father's death, that's a valid question, and I want to encourage you to be honest with your questions. But just remember: he wanted nothing to do with his father, and his mother wasn't going to volunteer the information.

Roger and Eve? I appreciate your prediction that this marked the end of their budding relationship. Maybe you're right...

The Super Chief pulled off the siding at Lamy and headed over the desert plateau toward Albuquerque, sixty-seven miles away.

After Roger left Janet, he went back to his bedroom to be by himself and decompress. He looked out the window, trying to come to grips with all that had transpired. *Why didn't Mom tell me the truth about how Dad died? What's the point? So much about her doesn't make sense. Why didn't I ever check out what happened to him? Was I wrong all these years about Dad? But he never wrote or made an effort to see me. Mom said he never paid child support. Was she lying about that too? What else did she lie about? Why have I spent so much of my life trying to get her approval, even after she's dead? Why did I ever throw that engine at him? What a great last memory. Are you ever going to forgive yourself for that one?–You were just a kid; get over it.*

Roger continued looking out the window as the train passed cows grazing in a small field. Seeing the cows brought back a memory of when he was seven in 1968. His father George had built an elaborate HO scale model-railroad in the playroom that filled the whole space. With the tracks surrounding them, young Roger sat on George Wickersham's lap, adjusting the speed control on the transformer. He and his dad both wore train engineer hats. Young Roger was ecstatic.

George then started to play a game by pretending he was a dispatcher trying to radio the engineer of the train.

"Hey, Engineer Roger, are you there?"

"Yes. This is Engineer Roger," the young boy responded.

"We have a report that Bessie the cow is on the track again. Go slow by the farm." George lifted young Roger off his lap and placed the boy back on the chair, so he could run around the other side of the set and place a miniature cow on the track.

"Sorry, Mr. Dispatcher. I can't hear you!" the boy said gleefully.

Young Roger pushed the control to full speed so the train pushed the plastic cow aside. They laughed, jumping up and down.

"Poor Bessie! Moo!" George said.

"Moo!" young Roger followed.

Back in the present, Roger continued staring out the window with tears in his eyes. He couldn't help but smile through his tears at the fond recollection. *Where did that memory come from?* he wondered. It was like a floodgate of repressed positive memories of his dad had been let loose in his mind.

Besides thinking of his dad, Roger continued feeling guilty about what he had said to Eve. He wondered when he would get the chance to apologize to her and how she would respond.

The conductor's voice from the corridor interrupted his thoughts "Albuquerque is our next stop. Albuquerque, New Mexico!"

* * *

It had been the historic custom of cross-country Santa Fe passenger trains, including the Super Chief, to stop for a few minutes in Albuquerque so passengers could stretch their legs. It also gave local Native American vendors a chance to sell jewelry along the platform. Mostly it was to fuel, water, and wash the train. Amtrak still continued the tradition up to the present day. So in respect to this tradition, and to service the equipment, the train stopped for thirty minutes in Albuquerque.

At Roger's suggestion, the BNSF and Amtrak took the opportunity to pay special tribute to some of their former employees. A large banner hung above a crowd of people gathered on the station platform. It read, "Thank you, former Santa Fe Chefs, Cooks, Waiters, Pullman Porters, Lounge Attendants, and Native American Tour Guides. BNSF and Amtrak."

Curtis, Wixie, Henry, Dasan, and other former staff stood at the podium. BNSF executives, Amtrak executives, Roger, and Dena stood nearby. A small crowd of onlookers, including Janet and Eve, also watched as a local TV crew covered the ceremony.

Curtis stood at the microphone. "We all spent over forty years on this train and never got down off our feet. It was hard work, sometimes thankless, but we worked with a sense of pride back then. Don't see that much today. I don't know what else to say, except thank you."

Tears came to the men's eyes as the crowd cheered and clapped. Roger looked at Eve in the distance, but she looked away from him, saddened. He wanted to catch up to her and apologize for his rude behavior at the earliest possible moment, but he had to honor his responsibilities until after the ceremony.

As the ceremony was winding down, Eve turned away with Janet and they strolled along the platform, looking at vendor displays of Native American jewelry.

Janet stopped at one of the stalls and looked at the turquoise pendants on display. She held one in her hand. It looked like the one bought for her from this very same platform in 1944.

On that day in 1944, with Ernest standing a few feet behind her on the platform, young Janet fondled a turquoise pendant that had captured her eye. He noticed her interest in it. Young Janet then put the pendant down and continued walking toward several other Native American vendors selling jewelry to the passengers. Ernest kept a couple of paces behind because of her wish to be more discreet. She was afraid people would talk if they were seen too much together.

"What happened to not caring what people think?" Ernest asked.

"I'm concerned for you."

"Let me be concerned for myself."

"Ernest, what am I going to do with you?" she whispered.

"Promise me, you'll be there," he insisted.

She paused and looked away, unable to respond. Confused, she then headed back toward the train entrance.

He followed close behind. "I'll be waiting," he said, looking at her sadly.

She hesitated and then continued walking ahead toward the sleeping car entrance. A porter helped her up the steps.

Older Janet was startled back to present day as porter Henry Wellington helped her up the train steps. Eve stood on the platform below, waiting behind her mother.

Roger rushed over to Eve. "Eve, please, I need to talk to you a moment."

She glanced up and saw Henry taking care of Janet, so she backed away from the stairs. "All right."

"Please forgive me. I didn't mean what I said."

"No. I mean, yes, I forgive you, but no—maybe we are fooling ourselves." A tear came to her eye. "It has nothing to do with what you make Roger. I'm not that type of woman."

"I know. I'm sorry I said it."

"But maybe it's not right and we were headed down the wrong path." Eve looked down and then turned back toward the stairway.

"Will you please still come to the Turquoise Room at ten?"

She paused but did not turn back to him. "I don't know." She proceeded up the train's steps.

"I'll be waiting for you," Roger said, as he looked after her. Optimistically, he went to find the dining car steward to make a reservation for the Turquoise Room.

* * *

The train picked up speed as it left the outskirts of Albuquerque and headed through the New Mexico desert toward red rock mountains dotted with greenery.

Roger caught up to Dena and Dasan in the Pleasure Dome. He sat next to Dena as Dasan went further forward and stood in the aisle, talking to passengers like he did in the old days as an on-board tour guide. Violet Briggs and Chester Young, also present, enjoyed listening to him.

Dena confided to Roger, "I remember how proud I was of him as a little kid, when I got to watch him speak to the passengers. He had them transfixed by his stories." Then she changed the subject. "Roger, I know I agreed to go on the whole trip through to Los Angeles, but I was wondering if it would be all right with you if I got off with my father in Gallup? I want to visit the res."

"Sure. There aren't many more things to be done that can't wait until later. It's more important for you to be with him. Have a good time."

"Thank you," Dena said as she squeezed his hand.

"I should be the one thanking you—for all the help you've been."

"Roger, your dad took care of us, you've taken care of us—it runs in the family."

She was interrupted as other passengers started pointing outside to the front of the train. A group of ten Navajo sat on a desert red rock cliff overlooking the Super Chief. A pickup truck sat nearby. They waved enthusiastically toward the train. The train horns blew in response.

Dasan, Dena, Roger, and the other riders waved as they passed the Native Americans outside.

After the passengers settled down, Dena called to Dasan, "Tell them the NASA story!"

"I haven't told that one in years," Dasan said with a smile.

"That was my favorite," Dena said.

"Oh, then please do!" Violet said.

The passengers nodded for him tell it.

"Oh, all right," Dasan said. "In the 1960s NASA had astronauts do training on our land. Legend has it, a Navajo sheepherder approached two astronauts in lunar spacesuits. The sheepherder asked if he could send a message to the moon with the astronauts. NASA officials thought it was a great idea and tape-recorded the man's message. NASA asked him to translate, but he said no. They asked other Navajo people, who all chuckled when they heard the recording, but then they also said no. Finally, with cash in hand, one Navajo man translated the message: 'Watch out for these guys; they come to take your land.'"

The passengers in the dome laughed.

When the train pulled out from Gallup, Dena and Dasan waved good-bye from the platform as Roger waved back to them from the moving sleeping car entrance.

* * *

Janet came out of her bedroom with her cane dressed in an old blue dress with a yellow rose on her lapel. She had gotten dressed and left the room while Eve was sound asleep, taking an afternoon nap. Janet started walking down the corridor toward the rear of the train.

When she entered the round-end observation car, a flood of memories came back to her from that exhilarating night in 1944. On her subsequent trips on the Super Chief in the late 1960s, these round-end observation cars had long since been taken out of service. Most of them had been squared off in the early 1960s so the Santa Fe could use them midtrain. As Janet moved toward the rounded, window-paneled end of the car, looking out at the breathtaking New Mexico late-afternoon scenery, she was taken back to that fateful night.

The lights were dim that night in 1944 as she walked toward the rear of the car. Ernest sat alone on a stuffed chair with his back to her, looking out the rear windows into the big, moonlit sky.

Ernest looked at his watch: 12:15. He looked worried but then felt a tap on his shoulder. He turned around and saw young Janet's alluring figure silhouetted by the bar lights behind her. Immediately he jumped up and offered her a seat.

"You made it."

"Sorry I'm late."

"I'm glad you're here."

"I almost didn't." She looked nervous.

"I know, but I'm glad you did."

She glanced around the observation car to double check that no one else was there besides the bartender. That confirmation, along with Ernest's smile, relaxed her.

A few minutes later, the Filipino bartender, Ricardo, picked up two empty cocktail glasses from their table as young Janet and Ernest sat taking in the romantic ambiance. Thus far, they hadn't said much. Their eyes did all the talking.

Ernest then noticed a vase on the table with yellow roses in it. He lifted a rose, and held it. Then he motioned to her to see if he could place the rose on her outfit. "May I?"

"More flowers? What's a woman to do?"

Ernest took the rose and carefully slipped the stem into her coat breast pocket with the flower sticking out. The two of them were close to kissing, but they refrained.

Afterward, she took a yellow rose out of the vase and slowly placed the stem into his suit breast pocket with the flower sticking out. She slid her hand down his lapel before withdrawing it, gazed into his eyes, and then looked away.

"There's something else," he said. "I hope you don't mind."

He proceeded to take a small box out of his pocket and handed it to her. She opened it. It was the turquoise pendant from the Native American vendor at the train station. She was melting in front of this captivating man.

Awhile later, they headed back to their sleeping car, young Janet walking ahead of Ernest in the corridor wearing the turquoise pendant. She got to her room first and stopped in front of her door. She raised her hand to the door handle and let it linger there. He subtlety reached out his hand and held her hand for a second while standing behind her. She froze, facing the door, and didn't move to open it.

He let her hand go before continuing several doors down to his room.

He turned, and they stared at each other. Two lonely souls were feeling the rhythmic motion of the train going clickety-clack along the tracks beneath their feet. A moment of decision ensued as passion and social taboo fought against each other in their bodies.

Still standing by her door, she pushed it in and held it open, looking at him. He looked back to make sure no one else saw them and walked up to her. They kissed passionately as they stumbled into her room and closed the door behind them.

Back in the present day, older Janet smiled as she thought about that evening and then became embarrassed as she looked at the passengers around her in the observation car. Seeing that no one was looking at her, she relaxed and settled into a smile again.

Outside, the late afternoon sun enhanced the colors of the rugged landscape, giving the rock formations a brilliant orange and red glow. The Super Chief went through a short tunnel and then glimmered as it rode back out into the sunlight.

A few minutes later, the train stopped in Winslow, Arizona, in front of the once-famous, newly restored, Southwestern-style La Posada Hotel. Originally designed by renowned American architect Mary Colter, the hotel hosted many of the Hollywood elite and political dignitaries from the 1930s to the 1950s. Hotel guests, staff, and spectators clapped as the train stopped briefly.

Janet smiled at the crowd. She remembered staying at La Posada once and was moved by the story of how Mary Colter, a woman ahead of her time, had designed the hotel in 1929. The hotel had opened right after the Great Depression, and even though Colter felt it was her greatest achievement, it never was completely finished due to lack of funds. It closed in 1959 with all her personally selected interior furnishings sold at auction. Janet recalled the profound words of Colter when the architect witnessed her treasure being destroyed: "Sometimes a person can live too long." Colter died a few months after the auction. Janet started wondering if the same could be said of her. She tried to break those dark thoughts by also contemplating how nice it would have been for Colter to see the resurrection of her dream hotel.

The train moved slowly forward on the flat landscape toward Flagstaff.

It could be you...

...in the Turquoise Room

on the

Super Chief

All private room streamlined train between Chicago—Los Angeles

Extra Fare —Worth it!

Chapter Twelve

DINNER PLANS

OK. Now I'll get back to your question about Eve and Roger...

Later that evening, at nine forty-five p.m., Janet sat up in her lower bedroom berth observing Eve, who looked frazzled getting ready for bed. Eve put her pajamas on inside-out, noticed her mistake, and quickly took them off before putting them on again correctly. Next, she let out a muffled yelp as she stubbed her toe climbing the ladder to her berth. Janet smirked, shut off her reading light, and made herself comfortable. They both lay quietly in the darkened room with occasional shafts of light moving over their faces as the train rocked on some bumpy track.

Janet finally broke the silence. "You'll always regret it if you don't go."

"No. I can't." Eve said. She turned over on her pillow and tried to will herself to sleep.

* * *

The Turquoise Room, located on the first floor below the dome of the Pleasure Dome car, had been busy earlier in the evening, but was now occupied only by Roger, sitting at a table by himself, and an older couple. Roger never liked sitting alone at a table in public. He always felt people were wondering why he was by himself in those situations—like he was now.

The couple soon got up to leave, which left him feeling even more awkward in the now-empty room. He checked his cell phone again: ten thirty p.m. Sadness began to sink into his soul as he lost all hope she would come.

On the wall beside his table hung a large framed picture of a turquoise necklace along with a framed poster. Roger stared at the poster, which was from a 1950s ad featuring a romantic photograph of a couple in the Turquoise Room with two candles between them. The ad read, "It could be you…in the Turquoise Room." Roger shook his head. *I guess it won't be me,* he thought.

Wixie entered and started clearing dishes off another table. He noticed Roger looking dejected. "Young Mr. Wickersham, should I tell the kitchen crew to close for the night?"

Roger had given up on trying to correct Wixie about his name. "I guess so, Wixie."

"That Rocky Mountain Trout sure is looking good tonight. You want me to put in an order for you before they close?"

Roger paused for a moment. "Sure. Why not?"

As Wixie headed out of the dining room with his tray, he stopped dead in his tracks at the sight of Eve in the doorway. She looked stunning in a beautifully styled 1950s gown.

Wixie smiled and turned back to Roger, who had not noticed Eve enter. "Looks like the kitchen is stayin' open!" Wixie said. Then he turned to Eve. "I'll be right back to put your order in." Eve nodded to Wixie before he left.

Roger stood and admired Eve's beauty. She looked more glamorous than he had ever seen her before. She was a bit flustered by his gaze.

"Sorry I'm late."

"It was worth the wait…seeing you in that dress. You look lovely."

"Thank you. Until ten minutes ago, I wasn't sure if I would come," Eve confessed.

"I'm glad you did," Roger said. "I wouldn't want to eat the Rocky Mountain Trout by myself." He led her to her seat.

* * *

Roger and Eve mirrored the couple in the romantic Santa Fe Super Chief Turquoise Room poster ad on the wall above their table, with two unlit candles between them. Two full glasses of champagne in front of them had not been touched, along with two plates of Rocky Mountain Trout.

"Maybe we are going down a road we shouldn't," Eve said. "It's bad timing with you learning about your dad…"

"That has nothing to do with what's happening with us," Roger said.

Eve paused to consider what he'd said but then continued her thought. "And…I do have to sort out things with Peter, and…you need to see if you're on the rebound or not."

"I'm not on the rebound."

"But you must have feelings for her?"

"Sure, but that doesn't mean I'm in love with her, or that I want to marry her." He took her hand. "Since the first time we met, I couldn't stop thinking of you."

"You couldn't?"

Just then they heard the conductor in the corridor: "Flagstaff, Arizona. Our stop is Flagstaff, Arizona."

While Roger and Eve continued their dinner, the train pulled to a stop at the station outside. An unexpected visitor stood waiting on the platform to board the train—Roger's former fiancé, Brook, with a small bag in hand. The conductor wasn't expecting any new passengers to come on board, but Brook used her alluring charm to convince him that Roger would appreciate the surprise. After a brief stop, the train pulled out of the station.

A few minutes later, Roger and Eve were sharing a chocolate sundae for dessert with coffee in the Turquoise Room. Eve's hand froze as she held out a spoonful of sundae in midair.

"You feel it too, don't you?" Roger asked.

"What do you mean?"

"The same feeling I had the first time I laid eyes on you at Union Station. Tell me if it's just me."

She remained entranced until she noticed the chocolate sundae dripping from her spoon onto the white linen tablecloth. She set the spoon down. She felt rattled. She paused and then hesitantly said, "I…I can't make any promises, but I feel it also."

Under the table, he reached out to hold her knee. This was her weak spot. They looked lovingly at each other.

She tried to hold back her emotion and desire. "Oh, you are dangerous, Mr. Storm-Wickersham."

They almost kissed, but then she mustered what little resolve she had left and refrained. "I think I better let myself out and check in on Mother."

Roger looked disappointed as she got up, and then he stood up also. "Wait. I'll walk you back to your room. I just need to settle the check." He looked around for Wixie, who was nowhere to be seen.

"No. I'll walk myself back." She was feeling confused by the intense passion she had for him, and she knew she wouldn't be able to resist taking things further in the heat of the moment if they walked back together. She had to calm down and think more clearly. "I'll see you in the morning."

"Text me when you're ready for breakfast," he said.

She nodded and pulled herself away. He looked after her, admiring her beauty. Then he sat back down to wait for the check.

Wixie entered momentarily and left the bill on the table. "Oh, boy, Young Mr. Wickersham," Wixie said. "I am feeling the steam from here. You better not let that one get away."

Roger smiled at Wixie's humor as he took out his wallet. Then he tapped his credit card on the table, pondering the reality of what Wixie had just said. Seeing Roger look like a distracted lover, Wixie gave him a hard time. "Are you going to keep tapping that, or do you want me to take it?"

"Oh," Roger said. "Sorry." He smiled at Wixie.

"Look at you!" Wixie said. "Yes, sir, love is in the air." Wixie laughed, shaking his head as he exited. Roger nodded in agreement.

As Eve headed back to her room, she passed Brook in the Pleasure Dome car vestibule, heading in the opposite direction.

"Excuse me, is the Turquoise Room this way?" Brook asked.

"Yes. I'll show you," Eve said. She then wondered why this woman wouldn't have known where the Turquoise Room was after being on the train for two days. She hadn't seen her on the trip before either.

But then Eve realized this woman did look familiar. She escorted Brook back to the entrance of the Turquoise Room, and then saw her rush up to Roger, who still sat at the table.

"Roger! Honey! I'm here!"

Roger stood, stunned. She put her arms around him and gave him a big kiss. Roger returned her hug out of habit.

Eve observed their long embrace and stiffened. As Roger looked over Brook's shoulder, he saw Eve standing there and tensed up. Brook turned to look at Eve also. At that moment, Eve lowered her eyes and left.

"Eve, wait," Roger said.

Brook then noticed two coffee cups on the table. "You were with her?"

"Yes."

He broke away from her embrace to go after Eve, but Brook pulled him back.

"Wait! Who the hell is she?"

Roger felt torn between chasing after Eve versus making things clear with Brook, so she would see it was really over between them.

"You called it off, Brook—with your flight to Italy."

"Well I've had time to think, and I changed my mind." She pulled him back to her. "You know you want me, baby," she said seductively. She distracted Roger for a moment, but he kept his resolve.

"I've had time to think also," he said. "It's over. I'm sorry. I need to go now."

Refusing to take no for an answer, she seductively kissed the side of his face. As she did this, Wixie entered and looked shocked, made an about-face, and exited.

Roger tried to politely break away from her again. "I need to go."

He started toward the exit, and Brook abruptly changed her tone. "If you go to her, that's it. I'll never forgive you for insulting me this way."

Roger stopped, turned back, and said, "That's your choice. I didn't ask you to come, Brook."

He left her standing by herself, in shock.

Roger hurried out of the Pleasure Dome car and into the dining car that led toward Eve's room in the forward section of the train. The dining car was empty except for a woman occupying one table toward the far end. As Roger drew near, he saw it was Violet Briggs sitting by herself crying. He tried to ignore Violet by walking briskly past her, but his quest to find Eve would be interrupted. At the doorway his conscience got the better of him. He stopped and turned back to Violet.

"Violet? What's wrong?"

"We had a horrible fight over dinner."

He walked back toward the table. "About what?"

"I just took for granted that he would want to move to South Carolina if things progressed, but he said he'll only live in Vermont. Do you know how harsh those winters are there? I'd turn into an ice cube. And then on top of that, I find out he likes to get dressed up as a Union soldier and go out on those reenactments of the War of Northern Aggression. My daddy would have a fit. I feel like the rug's been pulled out from under me…Oh, I wish I never came on this trip."

"Violet, let me see what I can do. I'll talk to him."

"No. It's best to leave well enough alone. I know it's not your fault, Mr. Storm—you meant well—but this trip was a mistake." Violet stood up to leave. "Thank you for your kindness, Mr. Storm, but I should go."

"Violet, I'm sorry you feel this way."

Roger looked after her as she walked away. *What's going on here? Nothing's working out,* he thought. He quickly continued his quest to find Eve.

* * *

Roger was out of breath when he arrived at Eve and Janet's room. He was surprised to find the door open, and he saw the back of Eve's head as she sat in a chair.

"Eve! I need to explain…" Roger stopped himself as he saw a doctor standing in the shadows and Eve nervously stroking Janet's forehead as Janet rested peacefully in bed. Eve glanced at him and looked to the doctor.

"Her blood pressure is a little low," the doctor said, "but I think she just needs to rest. The higher altitude doesn't help. I'll be back with an oxygen tank."

Eve nodded to the doctor, and he left. She stroked Janet's hair, and Janet reached out to hold Eve's hand.

"This trip is just what I needed," Janet said. "Thank you."

Eve smiled, and Janet looked intently at Roger, still standing in the doorway.

"Come in and close the door," Janet said. He did so. "Be good to my daughter," she said.

Eve blushed, embarrassed.

"I'll do my best," Roger said as he looked at Eve, but she wouldn't look at him.

Janet stared intently at her daughter and said, "Don't let this one go. It may never happen again."

Eve felt more uncomfortable and wanted to change the conversation. Before she could, Janet spoke to Roger. "I know you have a kind heart, Roger, like your dad." She paused. "Roger, who gave you the list?"

"I was told not to tell anyone, but at this point, what does it matter? He…said his name was Mr. Chapman. Does that name mean anything?"

Janet looked thoughtful…then shook her head.

Eve turned back to Roger and whispered, "You can go."

"I'm not going until we talk," Roger said.

* * *

Roger arranged for porter Henry Wellington to unfold a wall in Eve and Janet's bedroom to make more space. Certain double bedrooms could be opened into a double bedroom suite (sleeping four with two bathrooms) by the porter inserting a standard Pullman key into a keyhole located in the wall, which would release a latch so the wall could be folded back accordion-style on a sliding track. After Henry exited, Roger and Eve pushed their chairs back in the larger room to make themselves comfortable. Janet continued to sleep, now wearing an oxygen mask that the doctor had delivered. Eve observed her for a few moments and said, "We can go out for a minute. She should be OK."

They walked down the corridor to the sleeping car vestibule, where Roger opened the top half of the Dutch door. They looked for a moment at the moonlit desert while the wind caught their hair. Pent-up passion filled them both.

"Eve, I didn't know she would show up…"

"You're still in love with her; just admit it."

"I'm not." He wondered, *How can I get her to understand my feelings for her?*

She animatedly gestured. "I won't put up with another man who thinks he can fool me and who thinks it's OK to have other women on the side. It's so demoralizing!"

She started to shake nervously as the core of her vulnerability came to the surface. She thought, *Where did that come from? Now I'm going to really scare him off.*

"I'm not that guy!"

"How can I be sure?"

"I told her it's over between us."

She took a moment to let that reality sink in, but then thought to herself, *What are you doing? You need to figure out what's going on with Peter.*

"What am I saying? It's not fair of me. I don't know what I'm going to do with Peter."

Finally she looked back at him, and he looked yearningly into her eyes. All the questions were not answered in her mind, but she could not resist him any longer. She leaned into his chest. They kissed softly at first, then passionately.

Chapter Thirteen

THE REUNION

It's OK that you still don't think it was going to work out with Roger and Eve. Everyone has a right to their opinion. You've probably guessed I'm a romantic—that is true, but I'm also a realist. Regardless, let's not break the romantic spell of the moment...

Roger and Eve continued silently holding each other tightly as they glanced at the moonlight over the passing Arizona desert.

"Did you say something?" he asked, breaking the silence.

She shook her head. "I was just thinking about your father—how he brought people to their destinations when he was an engineer. You've done the same thing with this trip."

Suddenly, in the middle of nowhere, the whoosh of train brakes slowed the train to a stop.

"Is there a stop here?" Eve asked.

"No. There's not supposed to be."

The conductor stepped into the vestibule, holding his train radio, and looked at Roger.

"There's something on the tracks. The engineer needs you up front."

"Why does he need me?" Roger asked.

"Beats me," the conductor said. "I was just told for you to go there. You can get out here." The conductor opened the vestibule trap door, which turned into steps.

Roger hesitated, nodded to Eve, and descended the steps onto the railroad track ballast. Since the ballast sloped off at a downward angle near the side of the track, Roger walked slowly and unsteadily in his dress shoes toward the front of the train.

Roger saw a vaguely familiar figure climbing down the side engine ladder in the distance, dressed in coveralls, a bandana, and a cap, silhouetted by the moonlight. The engineer walked ahead and disappeared around the front corner of the head engine, out of Roger's sight.

"Hey!" Roger yelled out. "What the..." he said to himself. His walk turned into a jog as he headed toward the lead unit.

Roger arrived at the front corner of the locomotive and was surprised to find a surreal scene: the engineer, who had his back to him, was trying to push a cow off the tracks. The cow mooed.

"Push her from the other side," the engineer directed Roger. "Come on, Bessie!"

Roger ran up to help. He recognized that voice. They finally coaxed the cow off the track.

Roger waited, looking at the back of the engineer in silence. Could it be?

Yes. The figure turned slowly toward Roger into the engine's light: George Wickersham. He looked the same as Roger remembered. He had not aged, and he still wore his black-rimmed glasses. It was a special moment as a father and son saw each other for the first time in forty years.

"It's you...Dad?" Roger asked in disbelief.

"Hi, Son," George said matter-of-factly. "Don't see cows on the tracks much anymore."

"But you're dead! You can't be my dad. Who are you?"

Roger's whole body started shaking uncontrollably, and he felt as though his knees were going to buckle out from under him. He folded his arms to try to stop them from trembling.

"It's me, Roger. Allow yourself to believe. There's much more to life than what you're used to seeing."

"You've been up here the whole time?" Roger asked, incredulous.

"Got on in Lamy."

"This trip was all about you?"

"For you, Roger, and for the others," George said. "Each person has their own story."

Roger felt a strange peace come over him; his muscles started to relax, and he stopped shaking.

George wiped off his hands with a towel and walked toward the engine.

"Come up in the cab. We can talk."

Roger shook his head and obliged, climbing up the ladder behind his dad.

* * *

Roger sat in one of the two front seats as George sat in the other, running the now-moving train. The assistant engineer had moved to the cab in the rear unit to check on something. The moonlight shone through the windows, creating a mixture of light and shadows that gave the interior of the engine cab an otherworldly blue glow.

George took off his black glasses for a moment, revealing his kind eyes, to wipe off some dust. Roger seemed uncomfortable; there was an awkward silence.

"I don't know what to say," Roger finally confessed.

"It's OK."

A few more moments of silence passed.

"Why did you never show up again? You never even wrote."

George reached into his coveralls and handed Roger a stack of returned letters addressed to "Roger Wickersham." Roger looked at them, stunned.

"I wanted you with me, but in those days, the courts favored the mother. I was left with nothing but paying your child support."

"You sent all these?"

"I actually came to see you again," George continued, "but your mother wouldn't…it just became too painful to keep trying. I'm sorry; I thought maybe when you grew up, we could…"

"Why did you come back now?"

Rain started to hit the windows. George reached forward and turned a black knob in front of him, turning the windshield wipers on.

"I was given permission to come back because you needed to know the truth. Your heart's become bitter, like my heart did after your mother left. I didn't want you to suffer the same fate."

"But you beat her. I saw the marks. Why should you be bitter?"

"Roger, I never laid a hand on her."

"Right."

"You have to believe…"

"Why should I?"

George's attention was interrupted as a yellow over green signal winked on ahead. "Wait. We need to take this siding," George said. He reduced the throttle and applied a light touch of air to the brakes.

The Super Chief slowed to forty-five miles per hour as it entered the siding and came to a stop, waiting for a train coming in the opposite direction to pass.

While they were waiting, George turned to Roger. "I kept wondering where those marks came from also. I'd come home sometimes, after being away a few days on the railroad, and she would cover herself and try to hide the bruises from me. When I confronted her, she'd always say she bumped into something...but then I finally figured it out."

Roger looked into George's eyes and knew what he was saying. "Ken?"

"Him, and there were others before. I could never satisfy her, was never enough for her."

Roger looked on, bewildered, taking it all in.

"But I'm not here to pass judgment on your mother. We're all sinners, saved by grace. She tried to live her life the best she could. She loved you. I give her credit for that. But you also needed to know the truth..."

After a few moments, Roger asked, "Did you ever really forgive her?"

"It took years, but I finally realized her only fault was that she didn't love me. Can't make people love you. I finally let go. This is what this trip is about—for you to let go of the hurt, like I had to."

"I could never figure out how to love both of you at the same time. I felt I was betraying her if I showed too much interest in seeing you."

"It's OK."

"I even changed my last name. I was so angry at you." Roger's eyes became moist as he came to grips with his own hardness of heart.

"I thought for years you didn't forgive me for throwing the train at you in the station—that's why you wouldn't come see me."

"Are you kidding me? That was nothing. I had a lot worse things thrown at me over the years!" George said with a laugh.

Roger chuckled also. Their laughter died down, and George said, “If you need to hear it, Roger, I forgive you. Will you forgive me for not being there when you needed me?”

Roger almost cried and then nodded.

Just then, a passing freight train of double-stacked containers rushing east from their origins in Pacific Rim countries blew by them, rattling the windows in the cab. After it passed, the dispatcher in far-away Fort Worth, Texas, cleared the signal, and George notched out the throttle as the roar of forty-five hundred horses came to life.

As the Super Chief picked up momentum, George looked over to Roger. “Time to blow the horn,” his dad said. “It’s all yours. You remember: two long, one short, one long.”

Roger moved over toward George, raised his arm to pull the rope handle, and then hesitated as he looked at his father.

George smiled. “Don’t worry. I won’t try to tickle you.”

Roger returned his smile and pulled the handle. The horn blew, two long, one short, and one long. Roger then let go of the rope, and they rode together in silence.

Chapter Fourteen

SECRETS

What really happened with George and Marlene? You're intuition serves you well: George didn't tell the whole story but just enough for Roger to get the idea. And what about Marlene's relationship with Ken? Well, I guess there's no harm in going down a short siding, since you asked…

When George and Marlene first married, she liked George's thoughtful and loyal qualities, but those qualities soon began to grate on her, and she felt suffocated being in a monogamous relationship with him. She knew she could control him, which also made her less attracted to him. In addition, she became bored with his simple lifestyle and didn't like living in their remote house in Glorieta. And as far as his job was concerned, in the beginning, when he could only hold extra board jobs, and not a scheduled passenger or freight run, she never knew when he would be called to work or come home. He was wedded to the telephone, awaiting a call to work, so they couldn't go into Santa Fe much. She recalled the momentary horror when she had called the crew dispatcher to determine his ETA, only to be told, "Wickersham? He died at Gallup tonight. Won't be coming home." Only after she felt her heart drop did she recall that it was simply railroad-speak for running out of time in which a crew could work under the hours of service law. All these issues added up to her dissatisfaction with their relationship.

The birth of Roger in the first year of their marriage was an accident. At least she knew the baby was George's. She didn't see other men that initial year. But a few months after Roger was born, she got restless. When George was out on the road, working as a fireman or engineer, she would find her way into bars and carry on with the more "bad boy" types of men, from all walks of life.

She kept her secrets from George for the first couple of years, but one time he came back home unexpectedly a day early and found young Roger being taken care of by a babysitter he had never met. One of his coworkers on the railway had once mentioned someone seeing Marlene frequenting a local watering hole, Evangelo's Cocktail Lounge on San Francisco Avenue in Santa Fe, but George had passed it off as mistaken identity. However, when he found young Roger with the babysitter that night, he knew he had to go and find out the truth.

He walked into the bar and found her dressed in a slinky outfit, making out with a biker on the dance floor. The innocence in his eyes drained out of him as he witnessed his wife's betrayal. He drew closer, hoping it really wasn't her.

She looked up from her kiss and saw George staring at her. Ever the cool one, she nonchalantly released herself from the biker and whispered, "Gotta go, doll. My husband's spying on me." The biker looked at George and smirked.

George stood there motionless, not knowing whom he was angrier at—the biker or his wife.

Marlene came up to him, and picked up her purse to go. "Well, what did you expect? You leave me home alone out in the middle of nowhere. I need to have a life too."

"That's no excuse."

"Don't lecture me."

She walked out of the bar, and George followed.

On the ride home to Glorieta, he drove with a melancholy look on his face. She opened the passenger side window and tossed her windblown hair with her fingers. Unable to contain himself, he picked up the conversation.

"What about our marriage vows?"

"What about them?"

"We promised to keep our marriage bed pure."

"I wasn't going to go to bed with him. It was just a little innocent fun. Don't be so uptight."

"Don't lie to me. I'm not stupid."

They rode silently for the rest of the trip. George never mentioned the event again—and she knew he wouldn't. He couldn't handle her dark side. She couldn't handle his devotion to her. She needed a man who didn't need her. She knew he was the type of man who would be faithful and hope she would turn around.

One thing was clear: Marlene had a love/hate relationship with men. She had no problem attracting men. Her problem was that she couldn't stay loyal to a man who really loved her, and she always felt she needed to look elsewhere. Somewhere in her past, she must have been deeply betrayed. What else could explain why she couldn't let decent men like George love her? For that matter, she kept most people at arm's length. She could only give herself wholeheartedly to men she knew would eventually leave her or treat her badly. She couldn't help herself. Their unpredictability made being with them exciting, so she continued going "dancing" and having flings when George was away.

The way she would dance with these men in the bars gave some people the impression she must have been a professional dancer at one time. At any event, she was used to a more wild and exciting lifestyle, and her monthly flings would take the edge off her restlessness for awhile; however, for the last year, she'd been going through a severe case of a prolonged "seven-year itch." She realized it wasn't that she was just bored with George; she needed more from a man financially than he could provide. That's when she met her new beau, Ken. She found him at the more upscale bar in the La Fonda Hotel near the downtown plaza in Santa Fe. They felt an instant attraction when their eyes met as she entered the bar alone, wearing a revealing dress, and he sat at the far end of the counter, dressed in his business suit.

She came over and sat next to him. "Nice suit," she said.

"Nice dress."

Such simple words started a torrid romance that moved upstairs to his hotel room within a few hours.

By the time Marlene moved out of George's house, she and Ken had been seeing each other for six months, with many emotional ups and downs along the way. One night after Ken had too much to drink, he hit her when she said she wanted to wait a couple more days to leave George. Ken was tired of waiting for the right time and thought she was making excuses, while Marlene felt a tinge of guilt not letting George say good-bye to young Roger.

The next morning Ken was remorseful and promised he would never hit her again, but he was still adamant they were leaving that day. This was the incident that left the black-and-blue mark young Roger saw on his mother's arm as a boy. So while it appeared to the world that she was leaving an abusive husband, she was actually entering into a volatile relationship with Ken.

Despite wanting to leave her marriage, one thing she wouldn't do was leave her son. That was another odd part of her personality: when she had young Roger with her, she always found babysitters for him so she could go out on the town, but she wouldn't think of leaving him permanently with George. Perhaps that was her way of relieving her conscience. At least if she brought young Roger with her, she could tell herself she was a good mother. She had no problem lying to Roger about George, as well as many other things. She didn't feel there was anything wrong with lying, if it suited her purposes.

Marlene found ways to lessen Ken's violent outbursts over the ensuing years by monitoring his drinking. She couldn't, however, control Ken's wandering eyes. He started cheating on her a couple of years into their marriage, but she put up with it because he gave her the freedom to continue her escapades on the side also. It was a marriage of convenience; they stayed together, living two separate lives. They figured it was better to maintain the façade of a marriage, rather than having to bother with another divorce.

Not having any more children besides Roger also made their situation less complicated. In fact, Roger was out of the house for the most part once he went to boarding school in ninth grade.

Even with all of Ken's faults, Marlene encouraged young Roger to be like Ken when he grew up. She liked that Ken was competitive and had to be the best at everything. She would always remind Roger that airlines were the way of the future and that that was where the money was.

Ken was good to Roger when he did see him: he would do things like take him to air shows, build model planes with him, or teach him how to play with remote-controlled toy airplanes. Sometimes due to Marlene's prodding, and at other times because of his own insecure competitiveness, Ken would make subtle negative remarks about trains to Roger and remind the boy he was better off living with him than with his dad. Ken thought George Wickersham was a simpleton who was really going nowhere in his life working for a railroad. Regardless of his attitudes toward George, Ken showed interest in Roger and spent time with him; thus, the boy eventually looked up to Ken and inherited his negative attitude toward railroads. Ken also helped Roger get into his alma mater, Stanford, and of course influenced Roger to go into the airline industry.

These were the family dynamics Roger grew up with.

She came in on the *Super Chief*

How else would she travel to and from California?
For the Super Chief is one of the most glamorous all-room trains in America, filled with people who know how to travel and appreciate the best in travel.
It serves those famous Fred Harvey meals.
It operates on a 39¾-hour schedule between Chicago and Los Angeles.
The Super Chief is the flag-bearer of Santa Fe's fine fleet of Chicago-California trains which run each day.

SANTA FE SYSTEM LINES . . . Serving the West and Southwest

T. B. Gallaher, General Passenger Traffic Manager, Chicago 4

Chapter Fifteen

INTO THE NIGHT

I went on a little bit longer there about Roger's family background than I wanted to. I get easily sidetracked, so maybe it's best if you reserve any further questions until the end. Let's get off the siding and back on the trip…

After an emotional evening, Eve slept soundly in the upper bed while Janet lay awake in the fetal position in the lower berth. The oxygen mask was off her face, and she wore a yellow rose pinned to her nightdress. She held the turquoise pendant, staring at it with a longing hope from years past.

She remembered the end of her trip with Ernest in 1944. They walked slowly along the platform at Union Station, Los Angeles, side by side, suitcases in their hands, each wearing their yellow roses. She also wore her turquoise pendant and blue dress.

Suddenly she stopped. "Will I ever see you again?" she asked.

"My birthday is May 2; it's always been a lucky day to me. Promise to meet me on my first birthday after the war is over."

"OK!" she said. "Where?"

"Right here on the train platform where the Super Chief arrives, at eight thirty a.m."

"It's a deal."

"Remember, I'll always be the one with the yellow rose when the Super Chief arrives," Ernest said.

"And I'll be the one with the yellow rose and turquoise pendant."

They looked into each other's eyes for a moment, their fingers touching briefly, and then…they disappeared into the crowd.

Young Janet showed up as promised on the platform two years later, May 2, 1946, at eight thirty a.m.—Ernest's first birthday after the war was over. She walked along the platform expectantly, wearing her yellow rose, turquoise pendant, and blue dress. She had no suitcase, since she lived in Los Angeles. Right on time, the red nose of the Super Chief passed and the train eased to a stop in front of her.

She sat on a platform bench, looking around for Ernest. Gradually the train unloaded, and more people walked by. A man sat at the other end of the bench, but she saw no sign of Ernest. After a few minutes, the platform became empty again.

Except for the occasional short break away from the bench, she stayed waiting there until evening. She repeated the same ritual for the next two years, on May 2, 1947 and May 2, 1948.

As day turned to night for the third year in a row, on May 2, 1948, she looked around again for one last moment. She was the only soul on the platform. She rose to leave, finally realizing she had to move on with her life.

Back in the present day, Janet's eyes were closed in the sleeping car berth as she still lay in the fetal position. Her right hand turned over and went limp—still holding the turquoise pendant.

Eve, sleeping in the berth above, suddenly awoke as she felt a strange coldness in the room. Outside, the faint light of dawn shone through the window as the train moved through the California desert. She climbed down the ladder to check on her mother. She found that Janet had no color and her body was cold. She immediately called the doctor and Roger, who both showed up within five minutes.

The doctor tried to find Janet's pulse but then shook his head as he looked over to Eve and Roger. Eve, sitting on the bedside next to Janet's body, bowed her head, deeply saddened. Roger stood behind her and bent down to stroke her back to try to comfort her.

"I'm sorry for your loss," the doctor offered. "Her vital signs looked all right last night, except her blood pressure was low." The doctor patted Eve's shoulder, and she rose up and looked at him. "I'll be just outside the door."

"Thank you, Doctor," she said.

The doctor nodded to her and Roger before he exited and joined the waiting conductor and porter, Henry, out in the corridor. The door closed behind him.

Roger put his hands on Eve's shoulders. She reached back and held one of his hands.

"I'm sorry," Roger said.

"I think this is where she wanted to die. She looks so peaceful—even if her prayer was never answered."

Santa Fe
Super CHIEF

Chapter Sixteen

INTO THE LIGHT
UNION STATION, LOS ANGELES

There's not much for me to say here, except things aren't always as they appear. I know, faith is required from your perspective, and there's a lot of tragedy and sadness in life. There's a guy I know who got nailed to a cross. He said there would be trials and tribulations in the world, but He overcame and said there was something more.

Dreams don't always come true, like they didn't with Janet, and like I experienced as well.

But if life could be described as a rug, I found I lived most of my life only focusing on what the backside of the rug looked like, with all its messy stitches not making sense. It wasn't until later that I got a chance to see the front of the rug and the wonderful patterns that are there. When you get to where I am, you will see. But I digress. Let me finish the story for you...

Since they were just about an hour outside Los Angeles when they discovered Janet had died, the conductor called ahead for an ambulance to meet them at Union Station, Los Angeles, instead of stopping the train sooner.

Roger sat with Eve in her bedroom.

"I need to call Peter," she said.

"Of course. I'll give you some privacy." Roger got up to leave.

"Thank you," she said to him and squeezed his hand before he left the room.

When Eve tried to call Peter, he didn't answer, so she left him a message about what had happened. She also sent him a text message.

Afterward, she sat alone looking at her mother's lifeless body. It all seemed surreal: her mother was there, but she was not there. Eve had feared for a long time what it would be like when her mother died and how she would feel. Right now she couldn't feel anything. All she knew was that it didn't seem real.

"Mother, wake up," she said. "I miss you already. I hope you're happy now…I don't know what to do. You know I don't like change. You always said I was too independent and that I never would listen to you concerning men. Why should things be any different this time?"

Eve sighed and looked out the window. Then she directed her thoughts to herself: *What should I do when Peter arrives? I can't believe I'm thinking about this. I need to focus on Mother.*

* * *

Roger suddenly remembered he needed to speak to Chester Young before they reached Los Angeles, so he searched for Chester's room in the next sleeping car. Before reaching Chester's room, Roger slowed down when he saw Violet sitting in her room with her door open. Her bags were packed, and she looked ready to leave. She and Roger exchanged glances before he kept walking to the next door down the corridor, where he found Chester with his door open also. Chester sat in his seat, with his suitcase packed and ready to go as well.

"May I come in?" Roger asked.

"Sure," Chester said.

"I know it's none of my business..." Roger said and then paused. "But it is my business. I invited both of you on this trip."

"It would never work out. I'm a Vermont Yankee. Think I'd wilt if I had to live in that hot humid Southern weather. I wouldn't fit in anyway. Some of those people down there forget the Civil War's over...still flying those Confederate flags. She even has one in her attic."

"Don't you think you can work past your differences? You could spend your summers in Vermont and your winters in South Carolina."

"Hadn't thought of that," Chester said.

"Chester, I need to go. You do what you want. But if you don't go into her open room next door and try to win her back, you're throwing away something great." Roger raised his voice. "I heard someone say when you find someone you love, don't let them go. It may never happen again."

Roger stuck his head out the door and said loudly, "Did you hear me, Violet?"

"I heard you," Violet said from her room.

Chester looked up with surprise to find her listening, but hid his excitement when Roger turned back to him.

Roger kept speaking loudly. "Just remember how lonely it is without someone to love you. You've both been given a great gift. Don't pass it up."

Chester glanced at Roger but then looked down and shook his head. Roger left the room and walked back into the corridor. He slowed near Violet's room again and tried to make eye contact with her, but she sat stoically looking straight ahead. He turned and rushed back to Eve's room.

* * *

Roger knocked on the door and found Eve resting her head by her mother's side. When she heard him enter, she raised her head and sat back in her chair.

"The last thing I want to do under the circumstances is put any pressure on you," he said. "You said once that change is hard for you. I understand if you need to go back to Peter."

She couldn't answer right away and remained silent.

"Just tell me what you need from me. I don't have to be here when Peter shows up. Whatever makes you more comfortable."

"I don't know. If you would like to stay here for now, I'd appreciate it."

He held her hand, and they sat together in silence for the rest of the journey.

The Super Chief slowed as it approached the curve at Redondo Junction and passed all the Amtrak locomotives and cars being readied for their next trip. From the new bridge over the line to the ports, the Los Angeles skyline came into view. When the train pulled into Union Station at eight thirty a.m., two paramedics and two police officers waited along the platform. Along with them stood rail fans taking pictures and redcap porters with electric carts. A local TV reporter was also on hand.

Passengers started to disembark immediately after the train stopped, and the TV reporter tried to interview the modern-day celebrities as they walked down a section of the platform covered with red carpet.

Chester and Violet had obviously listened to Roger's advice and made up. They looked like two teenagers in love again as they strolled up the platform, their arms wrapped around each other and a redcap porter behind them.

Roger stayed with Eve in her compartment while the police and paramedics took care of paperwork and prepared Janet's body to be lifted onto a stretcher.

After most of the passengers had gotten off, the conductor came in and asked Roger to come outside and join in a group photo with the train staff. Eve nodded to Roger that she would be fine, and he promised her he would be right back.

On the platform, Roger joined Wixie Wilson, Curtis Gibson, Henry Wellington, Thomas Peabody, and other staff and executives.

He and the others put their arms around each other when the picture was taken. Then they shook hands and gave each other hugs.

Thomas Peabody took Roger aside and handed him an envelope. "Don't lose this. We'd be honored to have you on board in our marketing department. I'd like you to come to Fort Worth to discuss it. Will you come?"

Roger was stunned and then smiled. They shook hands. "Of course!"

"We want to keep this train going from time to time," Thomas said. "People will come to have this experience."

Roger said his good-byes and headed back to be with Eve. As he returned, Roger wondered what would happen if he were to organize another trip with the Super Chief. *What kinds of mysterious "coincidences" might take place for other people who come on board? Would Mr. Chapman show up again with a list of invited passengers? And where is Chapman? That was so odd that he didn't even get on the train. What was that about?*

When Roger got to the sleeping car entrance, he saw the paramedics wheel Janet's covered body down the ramp on a gurney. He joined Eve and held her hand as she followed her mother's body out onto the platform. A golf cart was waiting for Eve.

Late as usual, Eve's boyfriend, Peter, forty with dashing looks, approached Eve. He noticed her holding Roger's hand. "Hey," he said as he confidently cut in between them and gave Eve a big hug. She limply responded while looking back at Roger. It was an awkward moment.

"I rushed over as soon as I got your text. Lots of traffic," Peter said.

"Peter, this is Roger," Eve started to say.

Peter acted dismissive toward Roger. "Hey, man."

"Hi..."

"I'll take over from here," Peter said firmly to him.

Peter impatiently wanted to leave and quickly turned and whisked Eve away toward the empty seats on the waiting golf cart. Once seated, Peter put his arm around her, and the cart sped away. Eve turned back briefly and glanced at Roger. He waved to her and watched them leave.

Roger listlessly slumped on a bench, exasperated. *She'll go back to him,* he thought. *I don't stand a chance.*

He looked up the platform and saw someone familiar, standing by himself with a cane: Mr. Chapman, no longer in a porter's outfit but dressed in the same Navy officer's ensign dress uniform as Ernest from long ago. He wore a yellow rose on his lapel, and he was looking toward the sleeping car entrance.

Roger had a sudden realization and said to himself, "Ernest...Mr. Ernest Chapman."

Roger turned back toward the sleeping car entrance where Mr. Chapman was looking, but there was not a soul in sight.

Then...was it? Could it be? Yes. Mysteriously, as if out of a dream, Janet walked out in her blue dress, a yellow rose on her lapel and a turquoise pendant around her neck. She walked slowly up the platform and stopped when she saw Ernest. They both tried to hold back their tears.

"Janet!"

"Ernest, where did you go? I waited for you many times."

"I know. I was there each time watching you, from a distance, in a wheelchair. But I just couldn't bring myself to face you."

"What on earth…why?" she questioned.

"I was badly injured in the war. I couldn't bring myself to ask you to take care of an invalid. That, and the bigotry we would have faced. I thought I was protecting you."

"Ernest!" she shook her head, almost despondent.

"I know now, on this side, that our love could have conquered all," he said.

"You took away my chance to love you," she said with heartfelt hurt and frustration. They kept looking into each other's eyes—their looks speaking much deeper than words could tell.

"Forgive me?" he asked with remorse.

"Yes."

They hugged for a long time.

Roger looked at them, dumbstruck. After their hug, Mr. Chapman looked over to Roger and gave him a snappy military salute. Roger waved back with a smile. Then Ensign Chapman and Janet, arm in arm and walking with their canes on the outside, descended the ramp to the tunnel. As they entered the tunnel, they morphed into young Ernest and young Janet, without canes. They looked at each other lovingly and disappeared into the bright light coming out of the tunnel.

Roger looked after them with moistened eyes and pinched himself to make sure he wasn't dreaming. He had just had a supernatural glimpse into heaven. He thought, *What is going on? Oh, no! I almost forgot!*

He broke from his trance and realized he had almost forgotten about his dad. He immediately ran toward the front of the train, breathing heavily, fearing he had missed him. He was greatly relieved, however, to see his dad climbing down the engine steps, carrying a satchel over one shoulder.

A puff of steam awaited George further up the platform, ahead of the engines. Father and son faced each other.

"My trip ends here, Son."

An awkward silence passed between them.

"Roger…Storm, you've turned out to be a good man."

"Thanks."

They looked at each other warmly.

"Roger, I don't think a man can fully know how much his dad loves him, until he has a son of his own. Maybe someday you'll have a child and you'll know." George lifted off his Kromer engineer's cap and red bandana. He placed the bandana over Roger's head and lowered it down around his neck. Then he placed the hat over Roger's head and pulled it down snugly on him. They embraced.

"Oh, I almost forgot," George said as he reached into his satchel. He took out the train box with the engine inside from many years ago and handed it to his son. "I put it back together." Roger looked at it, moved.

George turned to leave, but Roger drew him back. "Dad…my name's Wickersham. I'm changing it back."

George looked at him, tears in his eyes, and nodded. Then he turned, walked ahead, and disappeared into the puff of steam.

Roger looked after him, still wondering if he was in a dream, and then turned back. He slowly moved along the platform, toward the rear of the train. No one else was there—just him and the Super Chief. He stopped and gazed to admire the train one last time, then resumed walking with his head down.

From the other end of the platform, a woman's figure walked toward him. Roger looked up and stopped. He had a glint in his eye and anticipation in his heart as he looked at the woman who had picked up the pieces in his life, much like she had picked up the pieces of the teacup he had dropped in Janet's nursing home room and the pieces of the model train he had thrown down years ago as a child on the station floor in front of his father. No longer was there a lingering stress evident in his demeanor as there had been before venturing on this train ride. As he gathered Eve into his arms, he was now a new man who experienced pure joy and freedom. She too, began a new chapter in her life, ready to be fully loved. They held each other for a long time.

* * *

Well, what do you think of my story? I can see if you feel it's too neat and tidy. Everything works out, like a typical Hollywood ending. Well what did you expect? The trip ended in Hollywood! Just teasing—I try to keep a sense of humor.

Let me just answer that point by saying you don't know what's ahead for Roger and Eve. They still faced many challenges ahead. You may think it's the end of their story, but it's just the beginning. And things didn't turn out great for Brook. She still had a lot of issues to deal with.

Yes, I do believe there can be healing with your own mother and father. That's one of the reasons why I told you this story.

Where do I fit into this story? I must admit, besides taking care of Roger and serving as his guardian messenger, I had some unfinished business on my part to take

care of as well—and I had to seek special permission for that.

What? You don't believe my story? And you still don't know who I am?

What if I maintain the story is true? I should know. My name is Mr. Chapman—Mr. Ernest Chapman, that is.

Yes, I understand. If you were to go along with this, you'd still have some questions...

How are Janet and I doing? I'm glad you asked. We're fine. But I must say she was surprised to find out our home isn't filled with harps and clouds—that it's much more profound and captivating—but I'm not supposed to tell you about that right now.

I hope you can see that with my visit, a bit of magic has broken into your humdrum reality. "For some have entertained angels unaware."

Why you? Why not you?

Tell me, do you want to start an adventure today?

Hmm...that's OK. When you decide, let me know. Or if not, maybe I'll have to be more persistent with you, like I was with Roger.

Afterword

People often ask writers of fiction how they come up with their story ideas. I'm fascinated with the creative process myself. So how did this story come about?

There were periodic times since taking a few introductory screenwriting courses in college, when I considered writing a feature-length screenplay, but I never followed through. 2001 was one such instance. I knew I wanted to write a story about the Santa Fe Super Chief and somehow connect an elderly actress to the story, but I needed to organize my ideas. One night I arranged to bounce some of those thoughts around over dinner with a friend who had a mutual interest in trains and films. As a result of our conversation, I wrote down a page of more focused ideas, and put them in a file folder. I soon turned my attention to other priorities however and forgot about writing.

Nine years later in 2010, I finally decided I would sign up for a screenwriting class and achieve that old dream to write a screenplay. As I was looking for story ideas, I came across that old file with my notes, but I felt there wasn't enough material for a feature-length story. All I had was an idea about an old white actress who gets on a tourist train and she remembers falling in love with a black soldier years ago on the Santa Fe Super Chief. They were to reunite later at Union Station wearing red carnations, but the man never showed up after he got injured in the war. It might have made a nice idea for a short film, but I felt it needed something more. So I was still stuck. I prayed for inspiration.

Soon after that, I thought about the story from a fresh angle and I got excited. I thought about how one of the best ways I connected to my dad growing up was when the topic was trains. Some of my best memories were from building train sets together and travelling with him by train across the country. I've been blessed over the years to this day with those shared experiences.

Then I thought: What if a boy grew up with similar experiences like I had as a child, but then his dad abandoned him when he was ten years old, and the boy grew up to be bitter and hated anything to do with trains? What would happen to him? In addition, I saw a story in the news about a mother who lied to her children about why their father had disappeared—that became the spine of my story and the project came to life.

I also wanted to find a way to actually bring back the Santa Fe Super Chief today and not just reminisce about it, so that is where the Mr. Chapman storyline came into the picture. I was able to connect him and a portion of the original idea into one of several sub-plots as well.

After I completed the screenplay, I wrote the novel. All I can say is that some story ideas can take eleven years to marinate.

Made in the USA
Middletown, DE
01 December 2020

25818665R00132